I0690534

Kiss Your Elbow

Kiss Your Elbow

An Embellished Memoire about
Growing Up in the 50's and 60's

Susan Stocker

Desert Palm Press

Kiss Your Elbow
An Embellished Memoire about Growing Up in the 50's and 60's

by Susan Stocker

© 2018 by Susan Stocker

ISBN (trade) 9781948327091
ISBN (epub) 9781948327046
ISBN (pdf) 9781948327053

This is a work of fiction - names, characters, places, and incidents are the product of the author's imagination or are used fictitiously. Any resemblance to actual persons living or dead, business, events or locales is entirely coincidental. All rights reserved.

No part of this publication may be reproduced, distributed, or transmitted in any form or by any means, including photocopying, recording, or other electronic or mechanical methods, without the prior written permission of the publisher, except in the case of brief quotations embodied in critical reviews and certain other noncommercial uses permitted by copyright law.

For permission requests, write to the publisher at lee@desertpalmpress.com or "Attention: Permissions Coordinator," at

Desert Palm Press
1961 Main Street, Suite 220
Watsonville, California 95076
www.desertpalmpress.com

Editor: Kaycee Hawn
Cover Design: Michelle Brodeur (eebowWORX)

Printed in the United States of America
First Edition September 2018

ACKNOWLEDGMENTS

First, I want to thank Lee Fitzsimmons for giving me a chance to share my story and believing in Kiss Your Elbow. Lee, you were calm and supportive throughout the process. Thanks also to Kaycee Hawn my editor for her knowledge and patience and Michelle Brodeur for the fantastic cover design.

Secondly, my partner of twenty-five years, Jan Cowin who has always believed in both me and the book. And for all the times I was in my office and not quite present, I'm sorry! Without your encouragement and support the book never would have come to fruition.

And for my writing group, Rachel Rudich and Jane Alden my great support team.

Dedication

To my mom.

In elementary school, Chris Chavez told me if you can kiss the end of your elbow, you get one wish. He said he wasn't sure if he'd wish for a puppy or a new bike. I knew exactly what I'd wish for.

Chapter One

I GUESS MOST CHILDREN think the world and their family revolves around them, like planets revolve around the sun, but this wasn't the truth in my family. My family was more like one of those bumpy, poorly painted, homemade, wobbly, and off-center universes created by some twelve-year-old for his science project. We all just banged into each other when someone moved the coat hanger.

My brother Randy was born at seven pounds-eleven ounces. A first-born son is always best, my mother once told me. Big brothers always protect their younger brothers. A family only needs two kids, she said. I think she meant boys.

They named him Randall David Webb, for my father's brother who died in infancy, and for someone else in my mother's family who had also died. I'm not sure the choice to have him named after not one, but two dead people, was a good way to start life, but Randy arrived, a photogenic baby with brownish-blond hair. He was both good-looking and smart, a perfect first-born son, and the Webb's happy life began.

When WWII came, my brother was not yet a year old. The Army drafted my dad and my mom went to work at Douglas Aircraft Company as a draftswoman. Someone had to watch Randy, and unfortunately for my brother, my maternal grandmother became his primary daycare provider. If there was any hope that Randy would end up being normal, it went out the window with that daycare arrangement. My grandmother would have affected the dead negatively. She was controlling, outspoken, and never missed an opportunity to make her thoughts known, whether you were interested or not.

Four years later, at one twelve a.m. on February 13, 1950, another child entered the universe. Because fathers weren't allowed in the delivery room in those days, my dad stayed in the car and slept through my birth in the parking lot of Community Hospital in Long Beach. My parents named me Susan, meaning a lily, and Lynn would be my middle name, for my father, Leonard.

By the time I showed up, my brother had morphed into this kid

1

with huge eyes on a face that had elongated to form a pinheaded child. A picture of us together shows me in my corduroy overalls in a high chair, giving the Power to the People fist, and Randy, who now resembled Paul Winchell's ventriloquist dummy, Jerry Mahoney, standing next to my chair. We looked like a ventriloquist act, he the scary puppeteer with giant eyes, and me the dummy baby, smiling my toothless grin, clueless how my life would soon begin to careen out of control.

The first time my sister-in-law, who's a nurse, saw this baby picture, she asked if the doctors had done genetic testing. She was serious. "Look at you. You're huge and look like you're from Mongolia!" She was unable to stifle her laughter. "Wasn't someone worried about how you looked?" She laughed harder. "You looked like you either had too many chromosomes or not enough. I would have been concerned if you were my kid!"

From the time I walked, at eleven months old, my mother's recollection was that I was in constant motion. She swore if she didn't hold tightly to my hand while shopping, I'd have left with any family who seemed more interesting than ours. Apparently, by her account, that was any family leaving the store.

By age three, Mom started to use a dog leash hooked onto the back belt loop of my pants to assure herself I wouldn't get away. I remember the leash; it was blue, and I could only wander about six feet away until I'd feel a strong tug, which meant I'd literally come to the end of my rope.

Martha Webb did everything in her power to have two of the politest, well behaved, well educated, and healthy children ever delivered on the planet. She was successful in most of those areas, with some of her offspring. She read to us for hours, helped us learn our numbers and letters, and encouraged our artistic expression. Using my drawing talent to create a life-sized barnyard mural of a farm on my bedroom wall with crayons was how my artistic talent emerged. This particular art project required my mother to wash the walls with a strong solution of Spic 'n' Span, prior to my dad having to primer it. Next, my parents had to repaint the wall with two additional coats of paint to block out the scene I'd so artistically created. My mother suggested chalk on the driveway for any future artwork.

We attended a cooperative preschool when no one had even heard of preschools. Both my brother and I were graduates and, of course, benefited immensely from this early school experience. I still have my finger painted, petroglyph-like drawings that Martha had lovingly written on the back, 'dinosaur,' 'lily,' and 'butterfly' as if later in my life, art critics would want to know what each piece represented.

Just before entering preschool, my body began to grow at an unusually rapid rate, turning me into a child giant. How this abnormal height affected me will unfold later, but it should suffice to say my sister-in-law was right—genetic testing might have been beneficial.

Susan Stocker

Chapter Two

I REMEMBER HAVING AN imaginary mouse friend named Mickey, who went everywhere with me. We had great adventures together in both my bedroom and our backyard and frequently carried on conversations. Mom even made him little tiny clothes, so he was always well dressed, for a mouse.

My mother, never wanting to stifle my creative side, made Mickey tiny pancakes from drips of pancake batter for breakfast, serving them on a little tiny one-inch round red plastic plate with a small plastic knife and fork that were gray to resemble real silverware. And, of course, she always put butter and syrup on his pancakes, because that's how he liked them. Randy consistently made fun of Mickey, and his teasing about my good friend caused me great anxiety.

"There's no mouse named Mickey that lives with you," he'd say, shaking his head.

"Yes, there is. You just can't see him 'cause he doesn't like you," I'd reply.

"Why doesn't he like me? 'Cause he doesn't exist, or because he's in your stupid imagination?"

"Shut up, Randy. Mickey doesn't want to hear you talk about him that way anymore, 'cause you're the stupid head."

"You shut up, 'cause you're crazy and you believe in an invisible mouse."

"Mom! Randy's bothering me. He's talking about Mickey again."

She'd tell my brother to leave me alone, and I was furious he'd question Mickey's very existence.

One morning, right after my fourth birthday, Mickey didn't show up for breakfast. He always came to Saturday breakfast when we had pancakes. His pancakes and syrup were getting colder as they sat there waiting for him. Mickey hated cold pancakes. Agitated and concerned about my friend, I couldn't understand why he hadn't come to eat with us.

"I wonder where Mickey is," I asked aloud as my mom walked away from the kitchen table with a load of dishes.

"Oh," said Randy, leaning towards me and whispering, "Didn't you know?"

"Know what?"

"He's dead. I threw him up on the telephone wires and he was electrocuted," Randy said with a smirk.

Mickey was dead? I was so stunned I could hardly breathe. The only way I could describe the sound coming out of my mouth was a deep wail from the bottom of my soul. Mother came flying back into the dining area expecting, I'm sure, to find either Randy or me in the clutches of some crazed, escaped, semi-human creature. Instead, she found me sobbing uncontrollably.

Snapping into commando-like action, she shouted at my brother to explain what had just happened. Randy, now scared by both my reaction to his story and our mom's reaction to me, also started to cry. Our mom, confused by this unfolding scene, was trying to get one of her children to give her a tidbit of information so she would know what offensive stance to assume. Obviously, something awful had happened, yet neither one of her hysterical kids could talk.

"Randy, what's going on?"

"Mickey's dead," he said blinking back tears.

"What are you talking about, Mickey's dead? He was fine yesterday," Mom said, still confused. Throughout this whole conversation, I continued to wail like a mortally wounded animal.

"I killed him, Mom. I'm so sorry," howled my brother in a mixture of fear and remorse.

"You what?" she replied angrily. "Why would you kill him? Have you lost your ever-lovin' mind, Randy? Why would you kill Mickey? Your sister loves her Mickey. What did you do to him?" She was now screaming at my brother.

"I electrocuted him," Randy admitted tears streaming down his cheek. "I threw him up on the telephone wires, and he was electrocuted."

"You did what? Oh my God! You threw him on the telephone wires and electrocuted him? Why, Randy? Why would you do such a cruel thing? Go to your room right now! You're grounded for weeks. Wait till your dad hears about this."

I was beyond being consoled. Mickey was gone, and I had to face a life without him. No more tiny pancakes and no more red plastic plate at breakfast. Thinking growing up was already getting hard, I had no

6

idea it would get harder.

While there were questions about my defective genes, my brother, on the other hand, would have benefited from early professional psychological intervention. Randy rarely spoke publicly and was called 'painfully shy' by his mentor, our mother. We were raised, as the old adage goes, to be seen but not heard, but Randy took it to extremes. Later, a kid like him would have been labeled lacking in social skills, or anti-social, but to our mother, he was just shy. Generally, he just stared with his big, wide-open, owl eyes, and never uttered a word in public.

Our next-door neighbor, Mrs. Bixler, owned a spider monkey named Manny. It was common for the kids in the neighborhood to go over to see Manny and to feed him the treats Mrs. Bixler left in a jar by the monkey's cage. Mrs. Bixler loved it when kids came over to see Manny, and when she would feed him treats, he would kiss her hand afterwards, leaving her cooing about what a nice monkey Manny was.

When anyone else gave Manny a treat, he would grab it, pop it in his mouth, and bare his little tiny monkey teeth back at you in a snarly "thank you." Every kid in the neighborhood knew two things about Manny. If you held on to the treat too long, he'd try to bite the hand that was feeding him. Secondly, if you stood too close to his cage and weren't paying attention, Manny would grab anything of yours he could. It could be your baseball hat, your shirtsleeve, or your grape Popsicle. Manny's cage was strewn with remnants of things he had grabbed from children. One time, my brother went over to visit Manny and apparently wasn't paying attention because the monkey grabbed Randy's t-shirt sleeve with one little monkey hand and pulled it into the cage. As Randy struggled to get the monkey to let go, Manny grabbed the collar of his shirt with his other little monkey hand. Now Randy was pulled up against the cage and couldn't get away.

Instead of calling out for help from Mrs. Bixler, who was in her kitchen doing dishes, Randy was so embarrassed that he wiggled completely out of his t-shirt and the monkey promptly pulled the entire shirt into his cage, screeching in conquest. Then, as if nothing had happened, Randy put his hands in his front pockets and nonchalantly walked home shirtless, which was something my brother never did in public because he was so bashful. To my brother, being outside without your shirt was about as horrible as being locked outside your house in your underpants.

Mom immediately knew something was wrong because of his bare chest and he finally fessed up that Manny had taken his shirt. She went back over to Mrs. Bixler's to see if she could get his shirt back and I could hear Mrs. Bixler saying from her driveway, "Why didn't Randy call out for help? Oh my gosh, I just feel terrible about this. Is he hurt? I just can't believe Manny would behave in that way. He's usually so sweet."

Retrieving the t-shirt from the monkey's cage was a hopeless cause; besides, the struggle and Randy's maneuvering to get out of the shirt stretched it out so badly, he couldn't have worn it again, anyways. I thought the whole incident was hilarious and grabbed at my brother's shirt like a monkey anytime Mom wasn't around. I couldn't believe my brother was so shy that he was embarrassed to cry out for help and let a monkey steal his shirt. Later, Manny would share a similar encounter with me, and I became much more understanding of Randy's decision to remain silent.

My brother and his best neighborhood friend Duncan, whom other kids nicknamed 'the Mute,' and who also rarely spoke, would create science experiments in our garage. They lit things on fire and methodically blew them up. They made a good pair, creating these Rube Goldberg contraptions they would swear could do all kinds of magical things. Wanting to believe my older brother could do incredible things, I loved the idea that he was able to create gadgets that, to a kid, bordered on magic. Once he told me he'd figured out how to make a broken household iron he found in the garage so hot that it actually felt cold to the touch.

"Hey, wanna see somethin' neat?" said Randy, poking his head inside my room.

"What is it?" I asked cautiously.

"Come on. I fixed something in the garage and now it works again, but even better."

"What do ya mean?"

"Come on and I'll show you," he said, heading towards the backdoor, with me in tow.

"Give me a sec, okay? It's gotta be plugged in." And with that, Randy picked up an old iron that had been sitting in our garage for years, climbed up on my dad's workbench, and plugged the electrical cord into a socket. Sliding back down off the bench, he said seriously, "Give it a few moments while it warms up."

As if he's an expert on irons, I thought. Then he spit on his two fingers like Mom did when she was checking to see if the iron had heated up enough and he lightly touched the bottom of the iron.

"Oh, yeah, it's heatin' up all right."

"Why am I watching you heat up an iron? What's so neat about that?" I said, turning to leave the garage.

"Wait just a second, okay?" With that, he spit on his fingers a second time and gingerly touched the bottom of the iron again. "Yikes!" Randy yelled, causing me to spin around, "It's really hot now! Okay, climb up on Dad's workbench and I'm gonna iron you."

"What are you, crazy? You've lost your marbles." I said and again turned to leave the garage.

"No, wait, I'm gonna say some magical words, and you won't even feel the heat."

"No way."

"Come on. Hocus Pocus, do my will, and no heat will she feel," my brother said intoned.

"No."

"Look." Randy ironed his own stomach. "The magical words worked; the iron's not hot!"

Against all of my better judgment and previous experiences with my brother, which were usually bad, I did what Randy asked and laid on my back on my dad's workbench and let him iron me. Amazingly, the iron was not hot to the touch. Okay, of course, the heating mechanism was broken and that's why it was in the garage in the first place, but I believed he had 'fixed' this iron and now could iron things and they wouldn't even burn.

Later, in the course of one of Randy and the Mute's experiments, they managed to blow up and burn one section of our garage. It was both exciting and frightening to see what boys could do with chemicals, matches, electricity, and no supervision. Psychological counseling, it turned out, would have been much cheaper than repairing the garage.

Susan Stocker

Chapter Three

I DON'T REMEMBER WHEN I first realized I wasn't like the other girls. After reading notes between my preschool teacher and my mother, someone should have recognized the multiple clues of a four-year-old.

"Susan only likes to play with the boys' toys," the teacher observed. "Susan continues to run over the other girls with her bike while playing with the boys." And the most telling observation from my mother to the teacher regarding my attire, "Susan only wants to wear her brother's clothes."

Always a foot taller than everyone else, I spent my entire school career, beginning in preschool and ending as a senior in high school, in the back row of all group photos along with the teachers and the custodians. This recurring event alone could have been fodder for years of counseling, always being relegated to the back row, but in many ways, it would end up being just one of my many worries growing up.

It was 1955, and everyone still believed their family was part of the Beaver Cleaver clan. Most families had both parents and two or three kids. Our family fit that pattern, except we had my brother the ventriloquist dummy who rarely spoke in public, and me the giant Mongolian child. We certainly didn't look like the average family. Because my parents were thirty-nine when I was born, if anything, they resembled most of my friends' grandparents. To make matters worse, my dad had very prematurely grayed hair, so it made him look even older. We just didn't look like any of the other families in our neighborhood no matter how you looked at it.

My hair was also always a problem. Strangely, it never seemed to grow well, and frankly, it was difficult to control as it stuck out in all directions. This was not at all acceptable in my mother's eyes, and so, taking matters into her own hands, she had me lie on the kitchen counter with my head in the sink and gave me my first, and only, Toni Perm.

I clearly recall four things about this incident. The counter was very hard, the perm stunk like a skunk, and the pink curlers were so tight they pinched my scalp. The fourth thing I remember vividly was witnessing my own transformation into a little white girl with an afro.

My mother had cranked my hair so tightly around those little pink rollers that my uncooperative nappy hair was now in a tight little brown afro, except for some hair at the back that accidentally came undone from the roller and didn't take the perm solution. There remains one photo from this incident and I look like I'm wearing some strange curly mammal pelt with a tail on my head.

By first grade, my mother made me grow my hair long enough to be held back in a ponytail. I hated it; I wanted short hair.

"Girls don't have short hair, Susan," she'd say. "You're not going to cut it," was the standard reply.

"I hate my hair," I'd tell anyone who'd listen.

One day, taking matters into my own hands, I took scissors and cut a section off the top of my hair to about two inches. Thinking this would force the issue and I'd get to cut my hair, I told my mom my hair got caught in a tree and the neighbor girl had to cut it out to save my life. She angrily told me the girl should have come and got her first. I told her I knew she wouldn't have been able to do anything, because I was hanging by my hair in a tree and the situation was critical; something had to be done immediately. Evidently, she didn't believe me because rather than getting the haircut of my dreams, my mother told me to go and put gel on the shorter part and just glue it down so it was part of my ponytail.

The hair gel in the 1950s was nothing like today's salon mousse. It was a slimy, pinkish gel called Dep, which was stronger than library paste and tasted horrible. If it got on your face and dried, it looked like snails had crawled around and left a slime trail. Once, at school, a kid drew attention to the fact there was dried gel on my face, telling everyone I must have fallen asleep in the garden the night before and the slugs got me. I socked him so hard in the stomach he vomited up cafeteria Sloppy Joe and milk on the playground.

It seemed no matter how hard I worked at it, there was always a shiny trail of gel somewhere on my face. It's hard to glue down the whole top section of your hair without getting some slime on your forehead, especially when you're in elementary school.

Besides hating my ponytail, I hated wearing dresses, and my mom made me wear capris or jeans with zippers on the side, which were known then as 'girl's jeans.' She wouldn't allow me to wear boy's jeans. "Boy's jeans are for boys," she would say. "You are a girl," she'd continue, with the emphasis on the girl part, as if this was a fact of which I was unaware.

Who cares? Girl's jeans looked strange and unnatural. Boy's jeans looked tough and cool. I didn't want to look or feel any stranger and unnatural than I already did and didn't want to be sentenced to wearing girl's jeans for the rest of my life. It seemed like there were no options outside of girl's jeans with their lousy side zippers. Flustered and annoyed, thinking I'd rather have short hair and wear boy's jeans, I'd retreat to my room for the hundredth time, and again try to kiss the end of my elbow—unsuccessfully.

Whenever I was able to get away with it, I'd sneak into Randy's room and dress in his clothes. One August, after Randy got all new school clothes, I was so envious of his new jeans that I waited for my mom to go to the neighbor's house before I tried them on. They were so stiff and smelled like new denim, I got a contact high just from wearing them.

I thought those jeans were so cool, with the front zipper and shiny brass rivets, as I walked around the house and looked in the mirrors. Feeling invincible and giddy from the denim smell, I strutted out into our backyard just as a bird flying overhead pooped. With my luck, a sparrow with an upset stomach just let loose on my brother's new school jeans.

Horrified, walking stiff-legged, and not bending my right leg, I hoped the bird poop wouldn't dribble any farther down the leg of the jeans. Hobbling back into his bedroom and trying to take off the jeans without smearing it any further was next to impossible. Frantically, I tried to wipe it off with a tissue, but that only smeared it more. My only option seemed to be to put them in the washing machine and wash the poop out, but then he'd know. Plus, I wasn't certain how one did a load of laundry, since my mom did ours, and the jeans wouldn't be stiff, new, and almost able to stand on their own power if they'd been machine-washed. I tried to wash the smear out with just water but that just made a larger ring of wet, whitish material. At a loss to what to do, I quickly folded them up and put them back in his drawer, imagining the moment he discovered his new jeans were tainted with white poop.

A few weeks later, he later pulled the pants out of his closet to wear, discovering the white spot. He bellowed, "Mom, look at my new school jeans. What is that on them? It looks like white goop. How could they have goop on them?"

Listening to this rant from my bedroom, I grabbed a book and pretended to read, but it was difficult to concentrate.

Immediately, my mom came to my door. "Do you know anything about this?"

"Nope," I said, shaking my head side to side quickly like a bobble doll.

"Are you sure?"

"I don't know nothin' about poop on his jeans." I feigned annoyance, head still bobbling. "How would I know about poop on his pants?"

"She did it!" my brother said accusingly, narrowing his eyes.

"Did not!" I shouted back.

"Then how do you know it's poop?" he asked.

"You said it was bird poop," I retorted.

"I said 'goop'," he replied, "Not poop!"

"Stop it, both of you," said Mom. "Give me the pants. I'll wash them."

"You don't know anything about this, right?" She repeated her line of interrogation, with emphasis on each word, pointing at me with her finger.

"No!" I wailed as if unjustly accused, facing a life sentence. I retreated to my bedroom. A second later Randy's contorted face appeared in my bedroom door.

"I know you did something to my jeans. You better watch out, 'cause I'll get you back when you least expect it."

For a moment, my heart was racing at the realization I almost got caught, then I began to giggle. I was satisfied I'd talked my way out of that situation, so I put my official Davy Crockett coonskin hat on my head, before placing my twelve-inch plastic hunting knife under my belt. I wandered outside to see who was around to play King of the Wild Frontier.

Seeing no one was available, I decided visiting Mrs. Bixler's monkey seemed like a good option. Manny was hooting and hollering like he often did, little monkey hand outside the cage demanding a treat. I got a pretzel from his treat jar and leaned in to give it to him through the wire mesh of his cage. Instead of grabbing the treat, he grabbed my coonskin hat right off my head and yanked it inside his cage.

It took me a few seconds to realize the furry object Manny had in his hand was my favorite, treasured hat. I was so mad but didn't know what to do. I quickly offered the monkey my twelve-inch plastic Davy Crockett hunting knife in trade, but Manny wasn't interested in the knife. He just continued jumping and bouncing from one side of his cage to the other while emitting an ear-piercing screech. He began to tear the hat into pieces with his little monkey teeth, throwing the pieces around his cage like discarded little dead animals. Then he alternately began rubbing the remaining fur hat in his hand gently on his face, or furiously on his crotch.

Manny was making so much noise, Mrs. Bixler appeared out of her kitchen with a piece of apple. The monkey stopped screaming immediately, dropped the piece of fur he was holding, and went to get the apple treat. Taking it gently, he then kissed Mrs. Bixler's hand in sweet gratitude.

"What was Manny upset about, honey?" asked Mrs. Bixler.

"I dunno," I blatantly lied.

"What was that thing he had in his hand?"

"I dunno," I repeated.

"It looks like it's furry. What in the world could that be?" she asked, just as Manny grabbed a piece of the fur and again began the rubbing routine between his face and crotch, focusing primarily on his crotch.

"Oh, my word, Manny!" she exclaimed. "Susan, honey, I think you better go home now, okay?" That provided me with the necessary excuse and I was gone in a flash.

A few days later, Randy asked me if I'd been over to see the monkey recently.

"Kinda recently, why?"

"Well 'cause now there's this ripped up fur in his cage that looks an awful lot like your favorite Davy Crockett coonskin hat, which, by the way, you haven't been wearing since the day Mom found the bird poop on my new school jeans."

"Don't know what you're talkin' about," trying to look innocent.

"Really? I bet you do," replied Randy. "Remember how you made fun of me when that darn monkey took my shirt? Well, now the joke's on you. Manny grabbed your hat too. Kinda embarrassing, huh?" Instead of mimicking a monkey and pretending to grab a hat off my head, Randy was quiet.

"I hate that monkey."

"Yeah, me too," he said.

We both grinned at each other.

Chapter Four

IN THE BEGINNING OF first grade, Rory and his family moved from St. Louis, Missouri, to Long Beach, California, and he became my best boyfriend. Rory had blond curly hair, super long eyelashes, and what his grandmother called 'a thousand-watt smile.' He was really good looking by any measure.

His family bought the house behind ours. He was one of the few boys my age in our neighborhood, and we were the best of friends from the day we met. Often, we'd met at the ivy fence separating our two backyards, to discuss the day, consider our options, and then make a plan. Sometimes the plans included other kids in the neighborhood; often it didn't. We liked the same things and we did the same things. I loved Rory, like a brother, like an equal, like an alter ego, the boy I could never be.

Although Rory was six months older, and a year ahead in school, we both played sports well and enjoyed notoriety in the neighborhood for being above-average athletes. We were a great team whether it was football or baseball. Loving all sports, we played almost weekly for years, after school and on Saturday and Sunday afternoons. He was the shortstop and I was first baseman. I was the quarterback and he was the wide receiver. We were a team. We were great together.

Because Rory was a boy, he could play Little League baseball. His parents took me along with his sisters to his weekly games, and I watched him wear his cool gray New York Yankee's pinstriped team uniform with envy. He played shortstop and I watched his team's first baseman miss his throws. I watched his team get third place, and I saw his disappointment and he felt mine.

We were both athletes, but because I was a girl, this relegated me to the role of cheerleader, audience, and supportive family member, rather than a star player. Bored and frustrated, I sat in the stands all season, in my Dodgers baseball hat, and ate overdone, rubbery hotdogs. He and I knew the reality; I was better than his team's first baseman, or right fielder, but because I was a girl, I was disqualified from playing

Little League. Everyone knew girls don't play baseball as well as boys. Girls were, well, girls, and therefore inferior to all boys in sports.

I don't really know who lost out the most during those years. I think me, but maybe it was every Rory in the world who never played sports with girls who were as good as or better than they were, and never learned it could be just as much fun. Rory and I regularly played both baseball and football in my backyard. Sometimes he made better catches and sometimes I did. It wasn't a boy or girl thing; it was just sometimes one of us played better than the other. We understood, we were comfortable, and we didn't see it as any big deal. Sadly, others did.

The first summer we met, we made up this game we called 'Little Boy, Big Boy.' The plot of the game was this: we were orphaned brothers living on a ranch where we raised pigeons and farm animals and rode horses. Our pigeon flock was comprised of red flowers from my dad's coral tree. When the flowers opened up, they looked just like red birds, complete with a beak, wings, and tail. We'd build houses, cages, and corrals to keep, raise, and protect our flock of birds, using plastic cowboys riding horses as our 'character' brothers. We outsmarted our enemies and lived the good life with our birds and animals, playing this game for hours on end, day after day, month after month.

Each day, we collected a new flock of pigeons that had fallen from the coral tree, and we created a new set of trials to overcome. We were always victorious over evil and always protected each other and our animals. We were a family. We were brothers. I was 'Little Boy' and Rory was 'Big Boy,' but most importantly to me, getting to be a boy character when we played this game made me happy.

It was the 1950s; kids played simple outside games and wouldn't have thought to ask to stay in the house and watch television all day. Though we played the regular games like tag and capture-the-flag, more than one game we made up and played was a little odd. We named one game 'push 'em off their bikes.' I don't remember who came up with the game, but we participated no matter how dangerous and nonsensical.

Actually, the stranger the game, the more the kids from outside our neighborhood seemed to want to play. Kids from blocks away, who we rarely played with, would arrive and join in these games. The rules for 'push 'em off their bikes' went like this: one group of kids lined up in the street, arms joined, forming a human barrier from curb to curb, while an equal number of kids lined up about two houses down the street astride their bicycles. Then one by one, the kids with bikes would start riding toward the other line of kids, gaining as much speed as they could, to try and ride through the opposing team's linked arms. For the kids linked arm-to-arm in the street, the challenge was to push the kids on bikes over, making them fall off, onto the street, resulting in a skinned knee or elbow, which became evidence of their failure and resulted in being sent to 'prison.'

Not every kid was pushed over or fell off. Some kids crashed into the curb, jumped off, or ran away. Those who actually fell off and were captured were taken to the prison in the Naylor's backyard until everyone on bikes had crashed, jumped, or triumphed by riding through the line.

The bigger kids who rode their bikes faster often got through the line, but if you were slow, small, or weak, you usually got pushed off your bike and often had a skinned body part as a testament to your failure.

One day, I made my biggest mistake ever in judgment in the history of the 'push 'em off their bikes' game. My black, three-speed bike received the previous Christmas was probably the best bike ever made, in my opinion, and I felt so cool shifting with the gearshift mounted on my handlebars. At some point, I thought it would be even cooler to mount the gear shifting mechanism on the right front fork of my bike, allowing me to shift gears with my right toe. What would be more impressive than a bike that changed gears by using the rider's big toe? Riding around our neighborhood, barefoot, casually changing from first to second, and then when I had reached the appropriate speed, into third gear, made me feel quite smug. I don't actually know if it was impressive to anyone but me, but I felt amazingly cool about my gear-shifting prowess.

The first time we lined up to play 'push 'em off their bikes' with my adapted gearshift system, I hadn't considered some things. Changing gears with my big toe required a lot longer runway to pick up speed, along with the fact that it required more dexterity than shifting with my thumb. I didn't think through the idea that my radical modifications would make it more difficult for me to succeed at this game.

When I rode towards the line of kids with locked arms, the first house only allowed me to get to second gear and I wasn't going nearly fast enough to break through the line of kids. The opposite team immediately picked up on my handicap, watched, calculated my speed, then broke ranks and ran full bore directly at me. While trying to get into third gear, my foot slipped and went into the spokes of my front wheel. I felt a sharp pain in the arch area of my right foot, and the sensation of turning a somersault, and then the bike came to a sudden stop.

I'd flipped over the handlebars and onto my back with the bike landing on top of me in the middle of Whitewood Avenue. As if that wasn't bad enough, they hobbled me off to the Naylor's backyard prison, and while I was trying to be friendly to the Naylor's dog, Winkie the Dachshund, the nasty-tempered little rat dog promptly bit me in the face. This required one of my few doctor visits outside of standard immunizations.

The doctor checked out my foot, declared it was bruised but not broken and suggested an ice bag. He then examined my left eye and face, put a gauze patch over the bite marks, collected his payment, and recommended no follow up treatments for either of my wounds. The bite mark scars were on my cheek for the next twenty years until they finally faded away. The bruised foot lasted a significantly shorter period than my bruised ego.

Chapter Five

KATY PALMER AND I were best girlfriends, from the day she enrolled at Mark Twain Elementary School and joined Mrs. Gaskill's second grade class. Katy was so petite compared to me that our friendship seemed odd from the beginning. Not only was Katy tiny and blond, but when she showed up her first day, she was instantly the most popular girl at school. On top of everything, she also understood how to tell time much better than I did. The teacher would test us by giving us a sheet of paper with just the hands of the clock on different times and we'd have to write in what time was indicated. This made about as much sense to me as the symbols on the Rosetta Stone. So Katy spent every recess in the sandbox, patiently drawing clocks in the sand with her finger, trying to help me pass the next time test.

"Come on, you'll get it," she'd say earnestly.

"But I don't."

"But you will. Just keep trying," she'd say again with endless confidence.

"All I ever get is cat poop I find in the sand." Both of us were uncontrollably giggling. "So two poops are two o'clock and one poop goes here like it's one o'clock? By now, both of us were on our backs, howling like hyenas.

Honestly, it was hopeless. I couldn't even remember on which side of the blank clock was three o'clock or which side was nine o'clock. Why did anyone need to know how to tell time anyways? You get up when it's light and you go to bed when it's dark. Seemed pretty simple to me.

Within months of her arrival in our neighborhood, a miracle happened. Katy, who was also a tomboy and had a ponytail like me, got a pixie haircut. Katy looked like a real pixie. She was small, cute, and the perfect candidate for short hair. I, on the other hand, did not resemble a pixie in any way, being a foot taller than all of the other children my age and built like a beanpole.

All I could think of the rest of the school day was how my luck had finally changed. Katy Palmer had short hair, and if she had short hair, that meant I might get short hair. My mom loved Katy. If Katy got a haircut, it had to be okay. Racing home after school to tell my mom that there had been a change in the local policy and girls do have short hair, I barged into the house with the news.

"Katy looks good, Mom. She has pert, easy to care for, short hair. Ya gotta see it."

"I'm sure she looks darling. She always looks cute," my mom said.

"I bet I'd look cute," trying to sound convincing. "You know I've wanted to cut my hair for forever, Mom."

"She looks cute because she is little and already looks like a pixie," Mom said, smiling, meaning I was not little or cute and did not resemble a pixie by any stretch of the imagination. I knew this conversation wasn't going the way I intended, since my mom was focusing on the small, cute, and pixie-like aspects of Katy. There was no way she was understanding my point of view. None of her adjectives would describe me, since tall, gangly, and unpixie-like were more accurate descriptions.

"Please," beginning to beg. "Please let me cut my hair, too." Then I revved up to a whine. "I really, really, really want my hair short, too. I hate my ponytail!"

"We'll see," she murmured. "Go do your homework and I'll speak with your dad."

Now we were talking. My dad could care less what my hair looked like. Things were starting to look up. In 1958, what father had a clue about what kind of hairstyle his tomboy daughter should have? Did Hugh Cleaver ever question the Beaver's haircuts? No. Did Doris Day's husband, David Niven, question anything about how their kids looked in Please Don't Eat the Daisies? No. Okay, so all the kids in those TV and movie families were boys, but really, dads were completely out of it in those days.

On the historic day I finally got rid of my ponytail, I remember these things: my mother took me to a hair salon, which was next to a tuxedo shop. It looked like a barbershop from the front, but when we got inside there was a woman who greeted us.

"Can I help you?" she asked unenthusiastically.

"She wants her hair cut," replied my mom in almost a whisper.

"Well, sit yourself down," she said, pointing to the chair and then, like a bullfighter, whipped the black plastic cape over and around me, fastening it at my neck uncomfortably tight. "That okay?" she asked, not actually interested in my reply.

"Yeah," I said, swallowing with difficulty.

It was over in less than a minute. The lady pulled my ponytail straight out behind me, and unceremoniously lopped it off.

"I want it in a ducktail cut," I said, as I'd practiced in my imagination many times before.

"Ducktail it is," said the hairdresser.

Suddenly I felt free, and in control of my own destiny. I was ecstatic. My mother sat quietly mourning not only the loss of my long hair, but also the loss of her dreams for me. I wasn't destined to be a ballet dancer or a baton twirler, but more like a softball player. I know that wasn't what she had in mind. She was now almost forty-seven years old and would keep my ponytail in her drawer for the next thirty years. The rubber-banded tress of hair would reappear a few years later when I was in junior high school, as my only option to ratting my hair like other seventh grade girls did. It would become my only ticket out of my mother's ridiculous rules on teenage girls' hairstyles versus split ends.

I walked out of the shop, felt the air on my ears and swirling around my neck. No more long hair, but a ducktail. Wait until Katy saw this. She in her pixie cut, and I in my ducktail—what a duo. The difference between our two new haircuts was immediately obvious. Katy did look like a pixie. I looked like a boy, a tall and skinny boy. I was elated. I could tell my mother was having another reaction to the shearing. She continued looking at me, while blinking rapidly. A growing horror began to dawn her face as the wheels in her brain turned. 'My daughter has just become my second son. What have I just allowed to happen?'

My father took it in stride as he always did. "You got your hair cut," he said very matter-of-factly.

"Yeah, Daddy, isn't it great!"

"So, you like it?" he said, nodding his head up and down questioningly.

"Yup, I love it!"

"Well, that's great, Susie Belle. I'm glad you like it."

My brother's comment went something like this. "You look like a boy. Why would you do that? Why did Mom let you do that? Jeez, you look like a spaz. Just stay away from me and my friends, got it?" He shook his head from side to side slowly. "God, you look stupid! Why'd they have to adopt you? They should've left you in the orphanage."

Having just cut my hair short, I didn't care about what my brother said. I looked pretty darn good, in my mind. Later that night, I overheard my mom talking to my dad while they were cleaning up from dinner.

"I had no idea it was going to look like this or I'd never would have agreed," said my mother from the kitchen, sounding on the verge of tears. I felt a little bad for my mom because she seemed so upset, but I really didn't get what the big deal was.

"Honey," replied my dad calmly, "just let her be. She'll grow out of this phase sooner or later. Just wait. It'll be fine. She's just a tomboy."

When I saw Rory the next day on the way to school, he took the change in stride. "Hey ya got your hair cut. I thought your mom would never give in. It looks good. I think it's shorter than mine," he said, laughing. "Wanna play catch today after school?" That's what I loved about Rory. No matter what, I was still just his best friend.

Getting rid of the girl's jeans was next on my list. That February, I got money for my eighth birthday, which was enough money to buy a pair of Levi's boy's jeans. Planning my defense, and arguing it was my own money, I reasoned it should be my decision what I decided to buy, and my decision was a new pair of boy's Levi's. Now I could smell my own denim jeans and stand them up in the corner of my own room. They were mine, I owned them, and in addition, I had the ducktail haircut to go with them. Life was perfect.

* * *

Katy spent almost every other weekend sleeping over at my house, or we spent the in-between weekends at hers. Katy had these young, attractive parents who started having their kids right out of high school. She had an older sister and younger brother, and her parents were active and fun. Their house was decorated and artistically coordinated and was really a showpiece, while ours was, well, boring.

Katy's mom was an artist and used unusual colors and fabrics to decorate. At Christmas time, she'd paint snow scenes on their front windows, which were better than the professionally painted ones on the MayCo's storefront windows. Their house had white carpeting throughout and splashes of bright colors. Our house was beige. The walls, the carpet, everything was beige. "I want to keep it neutral," my mom would say. Well, you're doing a great job at that, I'd think.

Ever since my mom bought the house herself, when my dad was overseas during the war in the 1940s, she wouldn't put any nails in the walls or hang lamps from the ceiling, because, as she cited dozens of times over the years, "We might want to sell the house later."

Somehow, holes apparently translated to a lower real estate sales price in my mother's mind. Katy's parents had art on the walls and swag lamps and all were associated with some kind of hole. Katy's parents apparently never intended on selling their home. Why sell it? It was such a neat house.

There were so many differences between our two families. My parents were old and out of it; Katy's parents were young, cute, and hip. She had an older sister and a little brother to play with. I only had my weirdo brother, and I mostly tried to stay out of his way.

The Palmers let me drink ice tea at their house, which I was not allowed to drink at home because my mom read somewhere tea would stunt my growth. The Palmers, who were all short people, joked that I needed to stunt my growth, and gave me all the ice tea I wanted. Mr. Palmer also once suggested I should smoke cigarettes because they also were thought to stunt growth, but he stopped short of actually offering me one of his.

They were such a funny little family and I loved to be with them because they were so much fun. They referred to my parents as 'L and M'—for Leonard and Martha—and knew how weird my parents were. My family was not fun in any way, so when I spent the night at the Palmers, we'd carry on until all hours of the night. I felt like I had fallen down the rabbit hole into a happy Family Wonderland. The Palmers teased each other and me and never got upset with us. Even the time I walked through their house with fresh dog poop on my shoe, leaving poopy prints all on their brand new white carpeting, they didn't get mad.

Twice I walked into and broke one of their swag lamps, because while they were all short and could walk under it, I was taller and would walk smack into it. They just teased me about being the Jolly Green Giant with dog poop feet. I think they were more used to chaos than my parents were because they had three normal children.

When Katy would spend the night at my house, my mother would monitor everything we did as if later she was going to write a report about her shift as our caretaker. To eliminate this scrutiny, we would close my bedroom door and proceed unmonitored. We usually spent this time mocking my grandmother and imitating my mother, but when we tired of that, we'd begin to think up other things to do to make each other laugh. The more outrageous, the funnier.

We went through one phase of putting an empty Coke bottle inside our pajama bottoms to imitate an erect penis. I still have no recollection of how either one of us had found out about erections or why we would know what one was, but apparently, we did because we thought the idea of this bottle simulating a penis was the best material ever. One of us would lie down and put the bottle in our pajama pants, then we'd make it begin to rise up like a penis until it was straight out and erect.

I would wag it from side to side as if it was a big snakehead until I was laughing so hard I could no longer control 'my member.' Then Katy would grab the bottle, put it in her pants, and jump up on my desk, pretending she was going to jump off and land on me with the bottle woody she was sporting. The bottle would, of course, fall out of her pants and land loudly on the floor and next my mother would be knocking on my door. We'd quickly hide it while my mother scanned my room for evidence of our activities. Finding none, she would just tell us to quiet down.

This game went on at every sleepover weekend at my house. We would become so bold with our antics that even when my mother would knock to come into the room, Katy would leave the bottle in her pants and slightly raise it so only I could see the bulge. Sometimes, she would even do this with my bedroom door open, at the last moment removing the bottle just before someone walked by. Spurred on by our success and growing confidence of getting away with these antics, we had a lapse in judgement.

More accurately, I had a lapse in judgment. Bored and lying around my room one Saturday night, we had exhausted all of our usual pranks and games and were looking for excitement. Even though the bottle game had become boring over time, it still managed to solicit more laughs than most of our antics. I decided I was going to put the bottle in my pants and then unzip my jeans and have it come out the fly as if it was escaping from my crotch. To accomplish this, I went into the bathroom, which was across from my bedroom, and positioned the bottle inside my pants, thinking it would pop out when my zipper was unzipped. To keep the bottle from dropping down, I had to lean way back, as if I was doing the Limbo, and balance the bottle on my pubic bone.

I got the bottle into position by leaning back, opened the bathroom door, and prepared to dash for my room. Running smack into Randy the weirdo and his sidekick Duncan the Mute coming down the hall spoiled my trick. Horrified, I tried to get past them before they saw my erection, but by then my body was trapped between the bathroom and the wall. I could only describe the look on their faces as terrified. Both of them froze, staring at this coca cola bottle coming out the zipper of my pants, as I continued bending backwards. Here was Randy's little sister, who already looked like a boy, coming out of their bathroom with an apparent erection, heading for her bedroom where her girlfriend was patiently waiting to be satisfied.

My brother's owl size eyes grew even larger and his mouth twisted into a horrible shape. If his eyes could have physically swirled in concentric circles, they would have, perhaps intermittently even counter clockwise. A loud and intense moan came out of his mouth that quickly turned into "Mom!"

Throughout the whole ordeal, Duncan the Mute, who had no idea what was going on, stood frozen in fear, staring at the floor. My mother arrived on the scene in seconds to take a report. By then, the bottled phallus had slipped down my leg and was wedged at the bottom of my jeans. Katy, aware of the disaster unfolding, came to the door of my bedroom to offer assistance as my accomplice.

My brother sputtered, trying to find words to describe what he had just witnessed his sister doing without saying the actual words. During his sputtering, Katy discretely removed the bottle from the bottom of my pant leg and hid the evidence. Randy was still trying to describe what had occurred to my mother without actually using the word penis or erection and was having difficulty. Duncan remained comatose and frozen, really wishing, I'm sure, he'd just stayed home and lit things on fire at his own house. Finally, Randy bolted from the hall, embarrassed and outraged, while Katy and I looked innocently at each other.

Chapter Six

RANDY, WHO WAS FOUR years older, had his own neighborhood friends, Charles Legg, Craig Lurd, Bobby Bonner, and Duncan the Mute. I didn't know much about Duncan and his family. His house was eight houses up the street from ours, with a poorly maintained lawn with numerous weeds, needing paint, and the living room blinds always drawn shut. The only thing that ever seemed to change was their trashcans would appear in front of the house on the morning of our block's designated trash day, and then they'd disappear sometime that night, as if some mysterious family member retrieved them. I don't remember ever seeing Duncan's parents; perhaps wolves raised him. Considering how anti-social he was, that wasn't such a far-fetched idea in my mind. It was no surprise to anyone that Duncan and Randy were best friends.

Craig Lurd lived a block north of our house on the same street. He was a cherubic Japanese-American kid, with a very light complexion and a multitude of moles, freckles, and a butch haircut. When he laughed, his face would turn bright red, and his eyes would disappear into his round, chubby face. Even his scalp got bright red when he laughed. Since Craig laughed at just about anything, we nicknamed him Cherry Bomb, 'cause he frequently looked like his head was about to explode. My mother particularly approved of Craig because he was so quiet and polite. She thought his parents had raised him right.

Charles Legg, or Chicken Legs, as we called him, was the product of parents originally from Kentucky. Charles' family looked like they were from the back woods and it appeared their relatives had unfortunately married each other over multiple generations. Charles had a skinny, pale, and almost translucent body. His dirty blond hair always looked like the family had just run out of shampoo when it was his turn to shower. His face had pimples, anemic freckles on the bridge of his nose and cheeks, and his clothes were always faded and too small. Charles always looked like he had accidentally worn his younger brother's jeans out of the house without realizing it or was ahead of his time and wearing clam diggers. He also always wore white socks that showed since his pants were too short.

Every summer, he'd get so badly sunburned, his nose resembled the beak of a turkey vulture: bright red and crusty. His mother had a perpetual vacant look on her face and was a dead ringer for an original resident of Appalachia. You'd swear she should be playing an autoharp on the front porch of a dilapidated shack with one hand, while balancing a baby on her hip with the other.

Charles' baby sister helped make the image even more real. 'Sister' was always perched on her mother's right hip like some pale, oversized growth. I'm sure his sister actually had a name besides 'Sister' but I never knew it.

The little girl had a constant frown on her face, and always appeared to be on the verge of a wail. Charles complained frequently that the toddler cried anytime his mom put her down, so she constantly carried the baby. Charles said his father held the belief the baby would end up lame because she wasn't using her legs, and his parents would argue about which was worse, her incessant crying or the prospect the kid would be a cripple. Charles mumbled that he personally voted that the better option was the kid being a cripple, 'cause she drove him crazy with her never ending crying, but I don't think he got much of a say in his sister's upbringing.

His father drove a black 1951 Chevy station wagon and was a bricklayer by trade. Mr. Legg's second job was to transport newly assembled coffins from Box Wood, Inc., a company that manufactured coffins, back to the Heavenly Chapel Funeral Home, which was our local funeral parlor, in time for the scheduled internment. In those days, nobody wore seat belts, so if Mr. Legg was transporting a coffin and the family had to go out, Charles and his younger brother Sam had to lie down in the back area of the wagon next to the coffin. When they drove by our house, the boys would lift their heads up to look out of the car, resembling a scene out of a horror movie, which always gave me the creeps.

One time there was some mix up at the funeral home and Mr. Legg was asked to transport not just an empty coffin, but a coffin with an actual body inside from another funeral home to the Heavenly Chapel Funeral Home where it was to be buried the following day in the cemetery. Because of the additional weight of the body in the coffin, Sam and Charles went along with their father to help load it into Mr. Legg's wagon. On the way from the first funeral home to the second, they stopped back by their house to pick up some paperwork Mr. Legg had forgotten.

This probably would have been unremarkable, except that evening, there was one of those rare California downpours. With impressive lightning and thunder crashing and rumbling through our neighborhood, our street quickly flooded from one side of the curb to the other. Unfortunately, Mr. Legg's black Chevy wagon, transporting the coffin and body to the Heavenly Chapel, stalled in the rain-swollen street in front of the house next door to ours, blocking the street.

The next sequence of events is somewhat vague, but this is what I remember about the unfolding scene. At about seven o'clock p.m., a bolt of lightning struck the large tree in the front of our house, lighting it on fire. The fire in the tree then lit the telephone pole next to it on fire, causing the electrical wires to short out in the transformer in a blinding blaze of bright blue light. That explosion left everyone's house in a one-mile radius without electricity.

When the fire truck arrived to put out the fire in our tree, it was raining so hard, and the streetlights were out, so the fireman didn't see Mr. Legg's dark colored station wagon stalled in the flooded street. The fire truck hit it head on. The impact caused Charles and Sam to sit upright in the back of the car and jarred the lid of the coffin wide open, exposing the dead body. Charles and Sam began screaming and tried to get out of the car. The fireman thought the car must also be on fire, so after rescuing the two boys, they began to douse the Chevy wagon with water.

In the commotion and darkness, no one seemed to understand what had occurred. I came out of our living room onto our front porch to see what was going on but was so scared and confused that I just sat down and leaned back against our front door to watch the events unfold. My dad had gone to choir practice after dropping my mom and Randy at his Cub Scout meeting for a mother-son Scout night, and my grandmother was baby-sitting me.

Remember, this was in the 1950s when Khrushchev was threatening to bomb the US with nuclear weapons. Our nation had become familiar with terms like radiation, atomic bombs, Cold War, and bomb shelters. We were all on high alert regarding our perceived enemies, the dreaded Russians.

At school, we practiced duck and cover exercises under our school desks on the last Friday of the month, while the city air raid sirens wailed their readiness. I didn't really understand what it was all about, but I'd overheard my mother voicing concerns to my dad about our own family's lack of preparation if the bombs actually fell.

My mom, with the help of my very paranoid grandmother, had put together a 'Webb Family Emergency Bomb Bag' that she felt would increase the chances of our family's survival should her worst fears come to fruition. Her family survival kit contained the following items: gauze, tongue depressors, Mercurochrome, four orange-colored baseball like hats with flashlights mounted on the visors, a mirror, a roll of tinfoil, and matches. There were also four gas masks from the local Army Supply store, a map of California, a camouflage pup tent, rope to tie us all together, and a pack of Wrigley's chewing gum. All of this was in a large duffel bag on which she had written WEBB in orange reflective tape on both sides, so we could use it for signaling some unknown force for help. My family was now prepared for any global emergency.

After the transformer exploded that rainy evening, my grandmother assumed the worst. The A-bomb must have been dropped right in front of 4315 Whitewood Avenue. As she had designated herself a first responder, she slung the Webb Emergency Bomb Bag over her shoulder and headed outside so she could be of help to anyone who needed emergency assistance. Flinging open the front door at full-speed and shoving the screen door outward, she caused me, who was leaning against the screen door, to be jolted sideways into our stucco porch.

"Ow!" I bellowed as the stucco scratched my arm. The flashing lights from the fire truck blinking red in the darkness outside only served to confuse my grandmother more.

"What are you doing? You'll get nuclear burns!"

"What are you talking about?" I asked more in pain than fear. I didn't know anything about nuclear burns, but I did know my arm hurt, and observing the Webb Emergency Bomb Bag over her shoulder, I knew something serious was happening.

Right at that moment, a car turned right onto our street, its headlights illuminating the orange-colored word WEBB on our family's emergency duffel bag. By now, the electric company was restoring power and porch lights were beginning to blink back on house by house. The rain had stopped and the car turning the corner was a familiar shape to me, our seafoam green Ford Galaxy 500. Thank God, my parents are home, I thought, so they could calm my grandmother down. In a few more minutes, she'd have had both of us tied together with rope, wearing Army-issued gas masks.

Randy was so mad he missed all the excitement, especially since he had spent the evening at a boring mother-son Scout meeting. Of course, he sat mesmerized in my room as I exaggerated the events to make them even more exciting. I told my brother the corpse in the coffin apparently wasn't actually dead and the cold water the firefighters sprayed on it revived it, and the man got up and out of the coffin on his own and began walking around like a zombie in a scary movie.

"No way!" said my brother.

"Yes way!" I said, "And if you're not gonna believe me then I'm not wasting my time tellin' you the rest. Get outta my room."

"Okay, I believe you! What else happened?"

"Well, as the previously dead guy got up out of the coffin and out of Mr. Legg's station wagon, he was then hit by lightning and his head exploded from all the 'embombing' fluid! Get it? Em-bombing fluid!"

"What? You big liar!" he said loudly, stomping out of my room as I fell on the floor laughing.

The next day's local newspaper headlines read, "Thunder, Lightning, and a Corpse on Whitewood Avenue in Long Beach." It was a headline we'd all recall in differing versions for years to come. Mr. Legg's car was declared a total loss, and the body was recovered still floating in the coffin and was later buried. The Heavenly Chapel Funeral Home said they no longer felt comfortable using Mr. Legg's transportation services, so sadly, he lost not only his black Chevy wagon, but also his part-time job.

Mr. Legg apparently had some kind of car insurance because about a week later he was driving an old blue Ford pick-up truck with a gun rack. Since the cab could hold only Mr. and Mrs. Legg and Sister, Sam and Charles had to lie down in the back of the pickup when they went out as a family. In the rain, Sam and Charles were rolled up in tarps like human burritos so they wouldn't get wet and catch colds. My mom said she was concerned the boys would either bounce out of the back of the truck if Mr. Legg turned a corner too quickly, or worse, wouldn't have enough air and would end up suffocating. Nothing ever happened to either one of the brothers, and they traveled this way until both boys moved out of the house many years later.

The last member of my brother's dorky friends was Bobby Bonner, or 'Boner,' as he was known when being teased. Bobby was an easygoing kid, overweight by nearly a hundred pounds, who bordered on being just plain lazy. He always wore blue jeans and a white t-shirt, which was two sizes too small, making the tires of fat on his stomach even more pronounced. His favorite saying was 'holy moly!' He lived with his mother, Betty, and his grandmother, Granny Bonner.

Granny Bonner had wild, grey, curly hair that shot out in tendrils. She wore high-topped black leather combat boots that laced up the front, wire rim glasses, used a cane to walk, and was known in the neighborhood to be a little off. She insisted she received telecommunications through a filling in one of her molars. Via this tooth, the Martians spoke to her, or so she said. Granny also lived in an army tent in Bobby's front room. Not in a bedroom, but in a pup tent in their living room, and at night you could see her shadow in the tent using a lantern to read.

Bobby said the reason she lived in the tent was because about two years ago, she heard through the filling in her tooth that Martians would invade the world, and she should be prepared. Hence the combat boots, which she not only wore during the day, but also slept in. She usually had a pair of binoculars hung around her neck to scan the sky at dusk, looking for spaceships, and then she'd journal what she'd seen. She apparently had boxes of journals inside the tent, documenting her daily contacts with these spacemen. Bobby said she told him the aliens would have strange-shaped bodies with multiple arms and be much more intelligent than those of us on earth, making it easy for them to invade us and our brains. It sounded to me like she should get together with my mom and grandmother, since they had concerns about the Russians ending our peaceful little life, and that was similar to a Martian invasion in my limited understanding of the world.

Bobby's mom had to take a series of buses to get to work at Woolworth's in downtown Long Beach and then back, which meant she was gone long hours Monday thru Friday. While his mom was at work, his grandmother was supposed to be in charge of him after school and summers, but her alcohol consumption and card playing, as well as her belief in aliens, made her a less than effective caretaker. My brother and I weren't supposed to go over to Bobby Bonner's house because of his grandmother, the liquor, the cards, and her lack of reliable supervision. My mother said I was a magnet for trouble, so his house was off limits. I don't think my mother even knew the part about Granny nightly scouting for aliens.

Chapter Seven

MY NEIGHBOR WAS ALSO named Susan Lynn, but she was two years younger than I was. When we were together, I was known as Susan One because I was the oldest, and she, Susan Two. We didn't have much in common, but if there was no one else to play with, I'd go over to her house and we'd hang out for a while.

Since I was the more creative, Susan Two would always ask me what I wanted to do, so I decided what we'd play, when to start playing, and when we were done playing. Susan Two also wasn't imaginative and didn't think fast like I did, so therefore, making up all the excuses and explanations to our parents for anything that went wrong while we were together also fell to me. She was so slow in making up the excuses that we always got caught red-handed and in trouble. Therefore, my main role in our relationship was to make up the lies.

Susan Two's older brother, Jerry, was a drummer in our high school band and I loved to play with his drumsticks whenever we played at her house. I'd find his drumsticks in his room and drum on whatever I could find that made noise. There was a large, three-foot diameter brass kettledrum in her family's living room, which served as a decorative coffee table. Whenever her mom wasn't around, I'd beat on the brass kettledrum with Jerry's drumsticks, loving the deep drum sounds. One time when we were alone, I was drumming away as if I was in a Marine Marching Band. Suddenly, the skin on the kettledrum split right down the middle from one side to the other. I stood there staring at the split skin and Susan Two turned to me with the 'what are we gonna say happened?' gaze.

"Fritz did it," I replied calmly. "It was Fritz's nails...he stood up on the edge of the drum and his nails split the skin." Fritz, their big, black standard poodle, was always getting into something, so he was the obvious source of this problem. Fritz, it was. That's what we said happened. Fritz did it. That was the lie, and another problem was solved.

In retrospect, I'm surprised I didn't permanently maim Susan Two, if not actually kill her. She was always the one I talked into doing things I knew we shouldn't be doing but went ahead and did anyway. Once while reading my brother's book, *William Tell*, I got a new bow and arrow set. These weren't arrows with some crummy plastic suction cups on the end, but arrows with guide feathers and metal tips. The kind of arrow that actually could pierce something—like Susan Two's head.

"In the book, the boy puts the apple on his head," I told her, "then his father shoots it off. Put this apple on your head and stand across the yard in front of the garage and I'll try to shoot it off." Now you're probably thinking this couldn't have happened, but it did. The first three arrows missed their mark, the apple on Susan Two's head, but the fourth arrow actually arched and glanced off her forehead, leaving a hole. Susan Two was apparently so shocked that I hit her with an arrow, she didn't even cry. She just stood frozen. Ecstatic I'd come so close to hitting the apple, and not noticing the hole in her head until I got up close, my comment was, "Wow, it made a hole in your head."

"My mom is gonna be mad you did this!" Susan Two said starting to cry.

"Then don't tell her," trying to think of how to explain this situation. Couldn't blame this on Fritz the dog. "Tell her you were swinging and hit your head on that bolt that sticks out of the swing set and it made the hole in your head. Besides, the hole isn't that big."

"My mom will think it's big," she replied, sniffling. "I'm gonna get in trouble for lettin' you do this to me."

"Then don't tell her, you dummy! Tell her what I told you to say, that you fell off the swing set and hit your head on the bolt. Got it?"

As usual, the bolt story worked, too. The hole eventually healed up and no one ever knew the real story, but from that time on, Susan Two was a little more cautious of my orders and didn't automatically do what I wanted her to do as easily. The Baby Girl Bagby incident, which happened next, was actually the last time Susan Two followed my directions and went along with one of my great ideas.

I had heard about Baby Girl Bagby for years when Susan Two and I were growing up. She didn't know what Baby Girl Bagby was, but she said she'd usually hear her parents talking about it with their friends after a couple rounds of martinis.

The first time I saw the wooden box on the top shelf of her mother's pantry, I didn't pay much attention to it because it was sitting beside the bags of flour and sugar and we were trying to make cookies. I noticed the box another time or two when getting something from the cabinet and wondered what it was, but never took it down to examine it. That was, until we were at her house alone, very bored, and the topic of the box came up.

"Why does your mom keep that wooden box up there?" I asked.

"I dunno," Susan Two said, shrugging her shoulders.

"You ever looked at it?"

"No."

"Let's...okay?"

"I don't know...yeah...I guess it would be okay."

Dragging over a kitchen table chair, crawling up on the counter, and retrieving the box off the shelf, I handed it down to Susan Two. It was about eight inches tall and maybe six inches wide, made out of polished wood, and dusty from being on the shelf for so long. Placing the box on the kitchen table, I opened the lid. Inside was a pink ceramic jar that looked like some of the vases my mom had our house, except it had a top on it. Pulling the jar out of the box and setting it on the table, both of us just stared at a shiny metal tag that read "Baby Girl Bagby" in fancy writing.

"This is the Baby Girl Bagby thing your folks talked about!" I said with increasing excitement in my voice. "What do ya think it is?" I was unable to maintain my composure; the idea of solving a mystery sounded exciting. "We have found the Baby Girl Bagby!" I announced aloud. "Let's open it!"

Always less adventurous, Susan Two quietly said, "I don't think it's a good idea to open it. I dunno why, but I don't think we should. My mom might get mad." At this point, putting the jar back into the box and returning the box on the shelf where it had sat for years unopened seemed an impossible request in my mind.

"I'm gonna open it." And with that, I pulled off the lid off the pink jar and looked inside.

"What's in it?" asked Susan Two, her eyes wide open.

"I can't see anything." I tipped the jar to the side to see if I could see inside better. "There's something inside of it. I'm gonna dump it out."

"No!"

"Yeah...why not? I can't even see what it is." With that, I turned the jar upside down and out poured a pile of light grey ashes onto her kitchen table. Eyes wide, we both stared at the pile, wondering what it was. I shook the jar again, listening to something rattle inside. I turned the jar upside down again and tapped the bottom of the vase with my palm; two little tiny grey bones that looked like old chicken bones I'd seen in the backyard incinerator fell out.

"Baby Girl Bagby?" I whispered. Susan Two was staring at the pile of ashes, too young to comprehend what she was looking at. For some reason, I, in my two-year older maturity, knew exactly what we were looking at. At that moment, I somehow understood opening the jar was something we never should have done.

Frozen in fear, and waiting to be struck by lightning, right there in the kitchen, we both sat completely still. With the evidence from my evil deed in a little grey mound on the table, I could envision the bolt of lightning and the puff of smoke right before I disappeared into a vapor, sentenced to an eternity in hell. I remembered my grandmother's prediction, "She's just not right, that girl!" and at that moment, I could understand her concerns. Maybe I wasn't quite right.

Susan Two still hadn't moved. She sat staring at the pile of ashes on the table, her eyes large, and her bottom lip trembling. "What is it?" she asked in a barely audible voice. For a moment, feeling responsible for not only the terrible results of my deed, but also for my little friend's shock, no words came to mind.

"It's...it's nothing," I said, scooping up the remains the best I could, and putting the ashes and the bones back into the jar. I put the lid back on the jar and the jar back into the wooden box. I wiped the remaining ash on the kitchen table off with the sleeve of my sweatshirt and crawled up and put the box back where it had been for years. We never again talked about what happened, but it was the first time I remember feeling guilty about something I'd done, and it felt bad.

Chapter Eight

IN THE 1950s AND 1960s, some parents—the mean ones—signed their kids up to the Don's and Deb's program at a local dance studio, which taught dancing and manners to boys and girls. Our mothers drove us to the studio, and then sat in a glass-enclosed area off to the side, where they could watch us suffer through an hour of dance lessons and proper manners. The Don's and Deb's program began in second grade, because by that age, everyone knew how to use the bathroom on their own. The program always began when school started in September and finished in June, just as school ended for the summer.

The first year, because most of us were seven years old and too young to be considered capable of learning either adult dances or manners, was called 'Country Kids' and everyone dressed up like cowboys and girls in western gear and learned simple country western dances. Of course, my mother enrolled me, and my friend Willy's mother enrolled him. We knew each other from church and school and our mothers decided it would be cute to make us matching square dance outfits. Besides that I wanted to be wearing jeans like all the other guys rather than a dress, I was horrified at the thought of matching outfits for one glaring reason; Willy was the smallest kid in second grade and I was already the tallest. Why this didn't seem to be a problem to anyone was strange, 'cause it was obvious to anyone with sight that we were not well-matched partners. Nonetheless, our mothers designed and sewed Willy and my matching dance outfits, and off we went to the first of nine lessons in Western dances. Willy, in his turquoise checked cowboy shirt, and me in my turquoise checked cowgirl dress.

It was pure torture. The instructors, all decked out in either cowgirl skirts, boots, hats, or jeans with red bandanas hanging out of their back pocket, were sickening in their over-the-top enthusiasm for the dances. All in a circle, ready to do the Texas Two-Step, the girls were supposed to curtsy, the boys bow, then everyone shouted, "hee haw," and the dancing began.

The first go-around the circle, the boys were supposed to lift their arms up, and their partners were to go under their arm and spin around. Willy was so short, I practically had to limbo under his raised arm, and it was totally embarrassing for both of us. Without missing a beat, one kid sarcastically suggested we switch places and I dance the boy part and Willy dance the girl part, but the instructor mercifully told him to be quiet. I made a mental note to shove him after class.

Twenty awkward second graders all tripped their way through the Cowboy Waltz in our offbeat clumsy ways, except a kid named Kenny who, for some mysterious reason, was a decent country western dancer for a seven-year-old. His partner, Sherryl, was equally good at dancing and they actually made it look easy. They were usually picked to give the demonstration of the next set of steps and Kenny would stand up really straight, look right into Sherryl's eyes just like our instructors did, and off they'd go Two-Steppin' around the studio.

Misery prevailed for everyone else in the dance studio, including my poor friend Ralph, who was so nervous about forgetting the steps that he'd have go to the boys' room to throw up. Ralph always threw up when he was nervous. He spent every Friday morning at school in the boy's bathroom because after the morning flag salute was our weekly spelling test, and while the rest of us would get butterflies, Ralph would have to barf.

While Ralph was in the dance studio bathroom, his partner Debby would have to dance the steps by herself, pretending she was dancing with him. It was weird to watch this girl twirling around and dancing by herself. Most of the kids in class laughed and giggled, and the instructors would glare and clear their throats at the kids who were laughing, and by the end of the hour, Debby looked like she was gonna barf too. I think they only danced one or two times together without some incident of Ralph having to excuse himself. This shared misery went on monthly for the whole school year with the accumulation of all the lessons ending in a big Hoedown with a souvenir class photo.

By now, my dress was way too small for me, having worn it for nine months and grown four inches taller. My mother left a very large hem in the dress when she made it, and almost monthly, she'd let the hem out. But due to my growth spurts and how much cotton shrinks, by the end of the year, there was no more excess hem to let out and my dress began to look more like an apron. Of course, Willy's shirt still fit him perfectly since he hadn't grown at all.

To start the festivities off, one of the overly enthusiastic instructors took the microphone, "hee hawed!" a few times and then began calling out the steps. We all got in a line with our partners, except Debby who lined up as usual without Ralph. By now, we had all gotten used to her dancing with an imaginary partner, so it caused far less stir. We had the souvenir group photo taken, showing all of us in our dance outfits with our instructors. As usual, I was in the back row with the adults, Willy in the front row with the midgets. After the photo was taken, we cheered that this particular chapter of our young lives was finally over. I hated Don's and Deb's.

Unfortunately, third grade Don's and Deb's would begin again the following fall and we started to work our way into the ballroom dances. Our instructors were now young adults. They were prior dance studio graduates who danced on the Lawrence Welk television show as professional, young ballroom dancers. Unlike any of us in second through sixth grade, who stumbled awkwardly through confusing box steps and sways, they made the dances look easy and fun. Again that year, most of our mothers sat in the glass-paneled gallery, allowing them to observe their suffering children learn the Cha, Mambo, and Viennese Waltz.

In third grade, we didn't have specific partners because we were still learning boy-girl manners. Switching partners gave us a variety of chances to practice our new skills. The boys had to wear a suit, tie, and dress shoes, and the girls, of course, dresses and flats. No girls could wear any kind of heel on their shoes because the studio's insurance wouldn't cover the liability if they slipped and got hurt. It made sense to me, 'cause I could hardly walk in my slippery new flats, let alone heels, and why would I want to be even an inch taller than I already was?

When we arrived early to class, kids ran and slid all over the studio in their slippery shoes or stocking feet. It was one of the very few benefits to coming to the class at all from my point of view. We whooshed around the polished wooden floors as if we were on ice skates. Little Willy Hamilton would sit on the floor with his hands tightly around his knees and we'd push him like a giant hockey puck and sail him across the shiny dance floor. This activity only lasted for a few minutes each week until all the students arrived and class began. Then we would get seriously down to the business of dance.

"One, two, three, one, two, three," the instructor would sing while we tried to waltz to the beat. We were still off beat and tripping into each other because most of the girls were trying to take the lead and the boys were so clumsy. The instructor would stop us and have us repeat, "One, two, three, one, two, three. Okay, try it again. Elbows up and in a box pattern everyone," he would say pleasantly. "One, two, three, one, two, three."

Couples who were concentrating on counting the steps usually forgot to watch out for the next couple and would stumble into them. This went on for an excruciatingly long period until we changed partners and began again to jockey for the lead again while counting.

I hated every session whether for the dressy girls' clothes and the shoes I had to wear or because I was the tallest kid in the class. I absolutely dreaded going to Don's and Deb's.

Chapter Nine

AFTER GETTING MY HAIR cut short in the ducktail, most people couldn't tell if I was a boy or a girl, and I was very happy. At the same time, my mother was very unhappy since admittedly, it was hard to tell my sex. The minute I got home from school, I changed from my school dresses into jeans and a t-shirt. Wearing Levi's with the popular tiny French cuffs, white t-shirts and black high-top sneakers, I played sports with neighborhood boys and could easily hold my own in our games. I actually played football and baseball better than most of the guys. I wasn't interested in being a boy, as much as I wanted to wear their clothes and do the things they did, at least at nine.

In the pecking order of the neighborhood, the high school boys would play baseball or football in the grass field across from our house, while the junior high age boys waited for their turn to use the field. Then, when both of those groups got tired and left, the rest of us elementary aged peons could use the field.

Every once in a while, one of the junior high guys wouldn't show up to play and they would ask one of the younger boys to fill in and play the position to make the teams equal. The possibility of getting to play as a substitute on the older kids' team kept many of us hanging around in hopes they would pick one of us for just such an honor. I had the baseball glove and hat and looked just like all the other guys hanging around and was dying to play with the older boys.

Finally, somebody didn't show up and I got to play in their game. It was like the 'ducktail haircut miracle day' to the tenth power. A day I would never forget. I took the field and played ball as if I'd never played before. I made every catch, even when diving for the ball, and I never dropped even one fly. When the game was over, an older kid said, "Hey, you're pretty good!"

"Thanks," I said, humbly staring at the ground. My status had been elevated and I was over the moon with excitement.

My brother was actually somewhat sports challenged. It wasn't that he couldn't play sports; it was just that I was simply better. He was older and wanted to join in the games the teenagers played in the field across from our house, but they'd never let him play. Sometimes we'd start to walk over to the field together, but once there, he'd pretend he didn't know me. They never picked him to play.

Late one afternoon, while home watching the Davy Crockett show on our black and white TV, Randy came charging through the front door in a fury, practically taking it off the hinges.

"My little brother," he grumbled. "They want my little brother to play. Not me, but my little brother." By now, Mom had come into the living room to find out what the noise was all about and found my brother seething with contempt.

"They told me I couldn't play, but to go and get my little brother because they needed a player to fill in the game," Randy said through clenched teeth, and almost in tears. My mother had no idea what he was ranting about, but of course, I did. Somebody didn't show up for the game and they wanted me to play.

"Sorry," I said unconvincingly, got my fielder's mitt and baseball hat, and left. My brother never got over that incident. He already disliked me, but now he wouldn't be seen with me anywhere in the neighborhood.

"You look like a boy," he'd say.

"So what?" I'd respond.

"You're not a boy and shouldn't try to look like one."

"You're just mad 'cause they don't wanna let you play with them and they'll let me." I screwed up my face. "You're just crummy at baseball!" I said, wobbling my head and shoulders, thus beginning a chain of events that always lead to a fight that had to be broken up, and both of us sent to our rooms.

"Creep."

"Moron."

"Loser."

"Idiot."

"Shut up."

"You shut up!"

By fifth grade, I'd perfected my male persona to the point that, when in a group of boys, it was impossible to tell there was a girl. The guys all just called me a tomboy, happy to let me join in the cat calls, and treated me as not only a peer but also a leader. Skateboarding had been introduced and mine was one of the first skateboards on the block. Better at skateboarding than most of my friends, I could also rebuild bikes better than any of the boys could and had an impressive amount of baseball and football equipment.

My poor mother had given up on trying to get me to be more feminine, thinking her attempts to make me act like a girl were futile, and my father, who was her only support, was oblivious to my unusual clothing and behaviors. My brother continued to either ignore me or beat me up, depending on his mood, which was generally bad.

Looking back, I can see how having a little sister who was not only better at sports but sought after by his peers as a team member, turned him sour at life in general at an early age. Over time, he became absorbed in lighting things on fire and blowing them up with the Mute, Chicken Legs, Boner, and Cherry Bomb, who were equally un-athletic and unaccepted by their peers. To me they were all just weirdos, but Mother referred to them as 'studious.' Either way, it's a miracle my brother didn't grow up to be a mass murderer, coming from our house. Particularly when you consider he already had big weird eyes like Paul Winchell's dummy and the growing frustration and anger to match.

He was bigger and would hit me hard when he got frustrated. He hit me in the head with a baseball bat and I retaliated by hitting him in the head with a golf club. I got a big lump on my head that didn't show, and he got twelve stitches above his eyebrow that did show. One time, he grabbed me by the front of my shirt with both hands, smashing my head so hard on my parent's dresser that I actually saw stars. My mother happened to walk by the doorway at the exact moment he slammed my head into the dresser. I dropped to the floor like a rag doll and laid still as if I was knocked out.

My mom cried, "Look at what you've done to your sister!"

"She's faking it," my brother replied, frowning.

"Faking what? She's unconscious!" Mother said angerly. "Go to your room now, Randall!" I waited a while and then began to moan, pretending to be coming out of my coma. The contact with the dresser really did hurt my head but getting my brother in trouble was worth it.

***

Fifth grade school year in the Webb House Rulebook meant bedtime was eight-thirty, Sunday through Thursday nights. My brother, who was older, had until nine-thirty. Randy would retire to his room after dinner, lock his door, and never come back out except to put in his retainer and put on acne medicine in the bathroom before going to sleep.

None of my friends had such an early bedtime and frankly, I was never sleepy at eight-thirty. I would say goodnight to my parents in the living room and then go to my room. It was too early to fall asleep, and I would make up games and things to do until I got tired. I used a flashlight to make shadows on the walls and read books under the covers, I had a stopwatch and I would hold my breath for as long as I could, and even listen to my transistor radio with earplugs, but none of these things held my attention for long.

Then, I started daring myself to do things. First, it was to get out of bed and see if I could take a few steps outside my room and down the hall towards the living room without my parents hearing me. Becoming bolder, I would take four steps outside, very quietly standing and listening to them reading the paper and watching TV. If they got quiet, I'd stand particularly still, hoping they would not walk around the door to the living room and see me standing there. A few times, they got up to do something and I slunk back to my bed, making as little noise as possible.

One night I was about half way down the hall when my mother said, "Go back to bed, Susan." Amazed that she had heard me; I decided the squeaky board in the hall gave me away. After a few nights, I decided to try it again and to avoid detection by stepping quietly over the creaking board, and it worked. Emboldened by my success, I'd sneak all the way up to the living room doorjamb and stand there, listening to the rustle of the newspaper my dad was reading.

A few times, my mom got up to go to the bathroom and I barely made it back to my room undetected. I felt confident, however; I could sneak out, and sneak back in, without either of my parents knowing. After mastering this, I started to think of more daring acts to do.

My first maneuvers were just a warmup in my adventurous game. The next time, I took the game to a whole new level. I snuck down the hall and was standing and listening to the television and felt an urge to do something risky. Unable to think of many things that fell into the risky category, I decided to moon my parents in the next room. Feeling bold I bent over, butt to the wall, and dropped my pajama bottoms, giving my parents a full moon through the wall that separated the hall between me and where they sat in the living room. The brazenness of my act so excited me, I could hardly contain myself. I mooned my parents with my naked butt in their hallway while they watched The Jack Parr Show! I had gotten away with it and no one even knew. This game was both addictive and thrilling.

Over the weeks, my parents did hear me a few times and told me to go back to bed. I obeyed and stayed in bed, thinking about what had gone wrong, and honing my plan to make sure it didn't happen again. Eventually, I snuck to the end of the hall, took off my pajama top, and stood there, counting the seconds. First, it was for only a few seconds and then for more. Taking off just the top of my PJs lasted for about a week, and then I progressed to taking off both my top and bottoms while standing there in the hall. This went on for a while, but then I started taking my pajama shirt off in my room, leaving it in my bed, and sneaking down the hall in just my pajama bottoms. You can see where this is going, right?

Getting away with doing something that crazy was exciting on some primitive level. Caught up in the excitement, adrenaline, and naughtiness of what was happening my perspective was lost on the whole event. While I enjoyed the excitement of getting away with something, this was reality—sneaking naked out of your room and down a hall to see if you could get away with it was bizarre to say the least. Unbelievably, and mercifully for my mother's mental health, she never did catch me naked in the hallway. Imagine what my grandmother would have said regarding that type of deviant behavior!

"I knew there were many things wrong with that child, Martha, but I never dreamed she would do something like that!" Worse, could you imagine my brother coming out from behind his locked door early to locate his retainer and see his little sister sneaking down the hall with no clothes on? Naked sister prancing down the hall; how much could one teenage boy take? Most of the rest of fifth grade was more normal for me. I lost interest in my nude hallway antics and moved on to other areas of creativity.

Our dog Queenie was the first thing I saw when I went out the back door in the morning and the last thing I saw when I had to go inside at night. She and I would roll up in a blanket on summer nights, looking at the stars, and she was always hanging around with me in the back yard. I loved my dog.

One day Katy and I were sitting on the side of our house, smoking dry daylily stems, pretending that they were cigarettes. Katy and I both liked to smoke the stems because we thought they made us look like movie stars with long dangling cigarettes with filters. It was there, hiding on the side of my parent's house, smoking dried lily stems, that we often came up with what we believed were our very best ideas and adventures.

That particular day, while smoking the dead stems, we came up with this idea. Let's dye my dog blue. Not the whole dog, we reasoned, just the parts of her that were white. That way the blue color would stand out better. What could we use to dye her? Food coloring, of course. My mother had it for baking and I knew where she kept it along with the cake mixes and birthday candles. What a great idea!

I went into the kitchen and got the blue food color bottle from the baking cupboard. We started by dripping the food color on the dog's white fur, but the dye trickled off, so we ended up using our fingers to massage the blue color in well. That way we would make sure there was good dye coverage. The white fur took the blue coloring well, as did our fingers, hands, and pants. When we'd finished, the dog was now brown, black, and bright blue. What a beautiful dog!

Next, we thought, how about dyeing my guinea pig, Spooky, who was also black and white. We put the remainder of the blue dye into a bucket and added water. After dipping Spooky into the water, she came out black and a lighter blue. What a beautiful guinea pig. We would have moved on to our cat, Kuma, who was completely white, but my mother must have seen the dog through the kitchen window and she began to bawl, "S-u-s-a-n -L-y-n-n -W-e-b-b!"

We all know that the use of our whole names meant something bad was about to happen in the next few moments. We ran from the side of the house to find Queenie bouncing up and down and my mother with a look of total disbelief on her face.

"What have you done?" she said looking back and forth between me and my friend. "Why is the dog blue? Have you two lost your ever lovin' minds dyeing the dog blue?" Her voice getting louder.

It was difficult to respond to her questions because of their rapid-fire sequence. For a split second, I thought of acting shocked, as if I, too, had just discovered the dog was blue, but my better judgment kicked in and that idea was abandoned. Mutely, looking at my mother with a blank stare, Katy to my right also stared straight ahead with eyes wide. Why had we dyed the dog blue?

"You, to your room," she said tersely pointing at me. "You, home!" She said pointing at Katy.

Poor Queenie got the short end of the stick. My mother refused to allow the dog into the house until all the blue dye wore off. Amazingly, blue food coloring on white fur actually has a very long shelf -life, even longer than my restriction.

Somehow, my grandmother found out about this incident and, in her usual omnipotent manner, again gave her professional opinion. "She's just not normal. Something is wrong with that girl. I'm tellin' you, Martha, you need to do something with her."

Susan Stocker

Chapter Ten

ONE AFTERNOON, MY BROTHER had his whole entourage in the garage working on some crazy experiment, when Katy and I walked by. It involved fire, electricity, test tubes, blue and green colored water, and a plastic pipe. They'd also concocted some terribly stinky, yellow, gooey liquid they were injecting inside of ping-pong balls with a syringe.

"What're ya doin'?" I asked.

"Nothing. Now you two need to split, like bananas," said Randy, causing the dorks to crack up.

"We don't have to leave if we don't wanna. Let us help too."

"Get out! You two should be doin' girl things anyways."

"Can't make us leave, and if girl stuff is so much fun, why don't you all go and play girl stuff?"

"Guys don't play girl stuff and you know it," he said, looking disgusted.

"Well, we wanna do what you guys are doing, or I'll tell Mom."

"Tattletale!"

"Okay, forget it. Let's just tell my mom, Katy, they won't let us play with them."

"God, okay, you can come in, but stay out of the way."

Apparently, the boys read about a similar experiment in some science magazine, so they found all the ingredients and readied their laboratory. The electricity was supposed to heat something, which then lit something else, causing steam to build up pressure in the plastic pipe. With the increasing pressure, the ping-pong balls were designed to shoot out of the pipe as if it was the barrel of a cannon. The ping-pong balls were supposed to hit a target Randy and his weirdo clan had taped on the opposite wall of the garage. The stinky goo inside the balls was not a well-thought out component of the experiment, nor, they'd discover later, were the other parts of the plan.

Once they assembled the contraption, Randy plugged in the electrical cord and we all stood and stared at the test tubes. Nothing seemed to happen. Then slowly, tiny bubbles began to appear in one of the tubes and a bluish fog began to rise. Soon all the containers were bubbling with blue and green liquid, and we were all transfixed, except Bobby, who had become bored and ended his participation in the experiment after the initial filling of ping-pong balls with the stinky liquid.

After a game of rock, paper, scissors, Charles won the honor of placing the first of the smelly goo-loaded balls tightly inside the cannon barrel, but he got so excited anticipating the ping-pong bomb firing that he forgot what he was doing. Craig, unable to control his enthusiasm, grabbed the first ping-pong ball and shoved it down the tube before Charles got the honor. This infuriated Charles, who grabbed the pipe back and loaded the remaining balls.

Suddenly there was a great bang as a small, white, circular blur exited the pipe cannon and headed towards Craig. Thwap went the ping-pong ball, smashing right into his cheek. The force of the ball hitting Craig's face cracked the outside plastic coating, and with his cherubic Asian-American face frozen in a grimace, he screamed, "Ow!" as yellow, stinky, rotten, cheesy glop dribbled slowly down his chubby cheek.

"Ha! Ha!" said Charles. "That's what you get!"

The first blast caused the cannon barrel to recoil so strongly it became slightly unhinged, so the second ball blasted out of the pipe in the opposite direction of the target, hitting my dad's shovel, knocking it loudly to the garage floor. The next blast hit the metal garage door with an ear deafening "Bang!" and Katy and I dove for cover. The stench from within the ping-pong balls was beginning to permeate the whole garage.

"Holy moly," shouted Bobby, more excited than I'd ever seen him, belly jiggling as he scooted down off the bench with a thump to find emergency shelter. Unable to fit under the garage bench because of his size, he grabbed the metal lid from a trashcan to use as a shield like a lumbering gladiator. "Pow!" went a ball again as it made contact with his shield. "Holy moly!" he shouted again.

Charles went into the Mark Twain Elementary School duck and cover earthquake position, his white socks glowing in the low light of my parent's garage. My brother scrambled, one arm over his head, trying to unplug the contraption, and Duncan the Mute was crawling on his hands and knees towards the side door of the garage in a futile effort to escape the unfolding scene. The odor was putrid!

Katy and I stayed on the floor out of range, hoping we wouldn't become the next direct hit. "Bang!" went the cannon again, now swinging wildly from one side of the garage to the other, hitting my dad's rack of screwdrivers mounted on the wall above his work bench, sending goo running down the garage wall. "Pow!" I heard, as the next one hit Boner's gladiator-like trashcan lid for a second time. "That stinks!" he gasped, burying his nose in his armpit.

The last blast brought my mother running from the kitchen. Banging on the metal garage door, she shrieked loudly, "What in the world is going on in there?" Randy slowly lifted the garage door open. "Is anyone hurt? What is that smell?" she asked, pinching her nostrils closed. Everyone was pinching their noses, trying to avoid the awful odor. No one said a word, as my mother tried to make sense of what had just happened. Frowning, she looked from face to face, trying to gain some insight into what had just gone on in her garage. No one was crying and nothing appeared broken, and besides the stink, there was no blood. Ready to begin documentation of the facts, my mom asked my brother suspiciously, "What's that on Craig's face?"

"We were doing experiments," my brother quickly admitted under her cross-examination.

"On Craig's head?" she said, cocking her head sideways and leaning in, resembling her own mother for a brief moment.

"Not exactly...he got in the way," said Randy, trying to sound casual.

"In the way of what?" asked my mother, cocking her head now to the other side.

"Of a ping pong ball..." said Charles, his voice trailing off.

Knowing this interrogation was going nowhere, she asked Craig if he wanted to use the bathroom to wash his face, but he declined. She left with her mental documentation in hand, which most assuredly would be filed away somewhere in her memory for further review at a more appropriate time.

"Just clean up the mess before Daddy gets home," she said wearily, "and please, get rid of that smell! Craig, have your mother call me if she has any concerns."

We cleaned up the goo and washed down the cement, while the boys argued back and forth as to who had caused the main problem with the cannon barrel.

"Those boys are crazy," said Katy, shaking her head. "They'd do better if they did play girl's games, since they sure messed up your garage!"

"Brain dead, in my book," I said, and we both laughed.

My brother and his friends' next experiment required actual fire department intervention. Randy and his dorks were crazy about rocketry. They drew rockets, they discussed rockets, they read about rockets, and they tried to build rockets. Duncan and my brother were even members of the Long Beach Junior Rocket Association. Craig's parents were pacifists and wouldn't let him participate in any formal organization that advocated rockets that could wield weapons. Charles' parents didn't have the monthly dues, so he didn't go to the meetings either. Randy and the Mute went religiously every third Saturday of the month as if they were training to build top-secret explosives for defense against the Russians.

They also attended the semi-annual club launchings at Hanson Dam, where the club members could fire off the small rockets they built. My brother would come home with drawings and blueprints depicting aluminum missiles, and he and his three friends would pore over the drawings for hours. They would ride their bikes over to the local library, check out any book or magazine remotely related to rocketry, and mull over how 'cool' it would be to actually build their own.

Finally, after many afternoons of discussion on all the details, they announced they were going to build their own rocket to launch into space. Randy, Charles, Duncan, and Craig pooled their allowances, rode their bikes over to the Douglas Aircraft Company's supply store, which was open to the public, and purchased the necessary materials. Bobby was too lazy to ride over with them but offered to help when they got back home. The four returned with one three-foot section of two-inch diameter aluminum pipe, a cone from some disassembled airplane part, and some type of mechanical device Charles was confident he could turn into the launching pad.

Using my dad's garage and tools, they sawed, glued, taped, and spray-painted all of the parts into this fairly decent replica of a rocket, complete with a homemade parachute, intended to allow the rocket to descend slowly enough so the launch crew could track and retrieve it for another flight.

They assigned Charles the task of designing the launching pad. Finally, he finished with what he was confident was a stable launching pad with the necessary pyrotechnic boost to send the experiment into the Long Beach sky. The only thing missing was the fuel necessary to launch the rocket.

The lack of this substance was only a temporary blip on their radar screens. Our dad had boxes of shotgun shells in our attic, left over from when he used to go dove hunting. The trick was to get the boxes down and out of the house before my mom figured out what they were doing. This is where I came into the plan.

"What're ya doing?" I asked, walking around the corner of the garage.

"Get out of here," commanded my brother.

"I don't have to."

"Get! Out!"

"Who's gonna make me? Are you makin' a rocket? Wow. Cool. When are ya gonna fly it?"

"As soon as we get the fuel."

"What kind of fuel?" I asked, surprised at his response.

"Gunpowder," Randy answered with authority.

"What? Gunpowder? You're an idiot!" I said, shaking my head.

"Shut up! We're usin' powder from Dad's shotgun shells."

"Dad said you could do that? No way!" I said, sure he was lying.

"Ah...no, but we could and he would never know 'cause he doesn't go hunting anymore. The shells are in boxes in the attic. If we get the ladder, we can crawl up and get 'em and nobody will know. We might let you help," Randy said slyly, "if you promise not to tell."

Randy and I had been up in the attic many times to look at this or that or to get things down. The space between the roof and the rafter floor was small and it was easier for me to move around than my brother, who would continuously crack himself on the head.

"Make sure you always walk on the supporting two by fours or you'll fall through the ceiling," Dad had always warned us. It was dry and musty up there with old hornets' nests in the corners. There were all kinds of things in the attic, most of little interest unless you were exceptionally bored on a rainy day. It's where my dad kept his guns and ammunition as well as my mom's old pictures and dusty treasures. There were some boxes of old papers and two broken lamps, but really nothing of any value.

To get into the attic, you had to get a ladder and enter through this rectangular space in the ceiling of the hallway between my brother's and my bedroom. There was a space of two feet by three feet to crawl into the attic, covered by a piece of wood that we could move to the right or left. The opening was too high for me to jump and touch from the floor, but my brother could jump and barely touch the wooden piece when he was showing off. He could even move the door closed little by little if he jumped enough times.

"We could do it when Mom goes to the post office this afternoon," I suggested. "You hold the ladder and I'll get the boxes of shells and throw 'em down to you. Bobby and Duncan can take them out to the garage and hide 'em, okay?"

"Charles can be the lookout," said Randy. Everyone murmured in agreement and the plan was set. With time to kill, we sat around the garage, imagining what the rocket was going to look like as it shot up into the sky. I was pretending to fly my brother's rocket through space when one of the black stabilizing fins fell, causing my brother to lunge at me.

"Cut it out, you jerk," my brother said. "Fork it over."

"I didn't mean to break it. I hope it holds up better than that in space," I said, feigning concern.

"Shut up!" replied Randy.

"You shut up!"

"No, you shut up!"

"Holy moly, you two. Both of ya shut your traps," said Bobby.

At about three-thirty p.m., Mom opened the back door of the kitchen, announcing to all of us in the garage that she was going to drop some letters by the post office and then she'd be right back. Trying to look nonchalant, we all nodded.

"I don't want any funny business. Do you all understand me?" She said.

We all nodded again.

"Ya don't want us robbin' any banks, right, Sarge?" I said, grinning.

"You know what I mean, missy. Don't get smart!" she retorted quickly. "I'll be right back."

By the time the seafoam green Galaxy 500 was out of the driveway, my brother and I had the ladder, and were heading for the hallway. Within moments, I had the wooden door slid to the side and I'd hoisted myself up into the attic. Bobby and Duncan were in the hall, waiting for the handoff, and Charles was by the driveway, ready to warn us if someone came home unexpectedly. In the dim light, I located the shotguns but couldn't see any boxes of shells. Twice, in the darkness, I slipped off the two by fours, fearing I'd fall through our ceiling like my father warned.

"Hurry up!" commanded my brother. "Mom will be home any minute."

"I can't find the shells. They're not by the guns."

"Just look around, you'll find 'em, but hurry," said Randy with a sense of urgency.

Finally spotting the stack of shell boxes, I grabbed three and toddled awkwardly back on a two by four over to the opening and the hall below.

"Here, take 'em!" dumping the boxes down the hatch to Randy standing below.

"Jeez! I can't catch that many. Be careful," replied Randy, frowning, as he handed the boxes off to Bobby and the Mute.

Walking back to the shells as if balancing on a tight rope, I grabbed three more boxes and crept back to the opening. "Here's more. Catch 'em! There're only three more boxes," I announced through the hole, and then waddled back on my balance beams.

I heard a muted commotion below but was unable to understand what they were saying because I was in the far back corner of the attic retrieving the final three boxes of shells. I finally deciphered that the voices were saying, "Mom's home!"

Popping up in the attic hole like a gopher, my brother said, "Hurry up! Come on! Get down!"

Moving towards the opening and trying not to fall off the beam or drop the last three boxes of shells, I got to the opening just in time to see the ladder disappear around the corner of the hall towards the garage.

Aw, shoot, I thought. I'd gotten down from the attic before by hanging by my hands and dropping to the floor below, but that was impossible while holding the remaining three shell boxes. I could drop the shell boxes, hang, and drop, I thought frantically, but if the boxes hit the floor and came open, the shells would spill everywhere. Hearing my mom's keys in the front door, I panicked. Slinking back into the attic, I put the shells down and slid the attic door shut with a thud. Now what? Shit. Shit. Shit!

There were muffled voices coming from the house below me, though I couldn't tell what they were saying until they were in the hall right under me.

"Where's your sister?" asked my mother from below.

"I dunno. We're just gonna hang out in my room, okay?" replied Randy.

There was a murmur of voices from where my brother's room was located, and my mom was in the kitchen, which was on the other side of the house. I quietly crawled over to the area above my brother's room and tapped lightly on the drywall below me that was the ceiling of his room. The voices hushed and then, after a few moments, there was tapping back. I tapped back again, in acknowledgement that I was indeed still in the attic and needed to be rescued. Then there was raucous laughter and multiple taps, and more laughter.

What a dickhead. More taps and more laughter. Eventually, I heard a tap on the attic door, so I made my way back to the door and opened it slightly.

"Get me out of here," I whispered. "I swear I'm gonna kill you, Randy. I swear to God!"

"Hey, hey," said my brother jovially, "Is that any way to talk to your rescuer?"

Opening the door a little wider, "Here, take the rest of the shells," practically dropping them on his head.

"Hey, knock it off," he whispered loudly, "or you'll never get down."

"I swear to God, Randy, get me down now or I'll tell Mom what you're up to."

"Why would ya want to tell, you spaz, you'll get in trouble too!" he whispered again, increasingly annoyed. "Hold on, okay, okay...wait a sec..."

By now, I was hot and mad. Opening the attic door completely and moving my body around, I hung down, and dropped to the floor with a dull thud. Looking surprised, Duncan, Charles, and Bobby stuck their heads out the door of my brother's room to see what caused the noise.

"I'm done. Tell Randy to shut the attic door." I looked up at the black, gaping hole. "You're a bunch of donkey butts." I went into my room and slammed the door shut, as the dork pod giggled uncontrollably.

"What's all the racket?" my mom shouted from the kitchen.

"Nothing, Mom," shouted my brother. "Nothing." Then I heard him repeatedly jumping to close the attic door. Assholes. My brother must have felt a little bad about how he hung me out to dry, leaving me in the attic, because he asked me and Katy to join them in the garage to empty the shell casings.

"Well, ya did such a good job at getting the shells down for us, I thought you and Katy might like to help with the rest of the project."

"I thought you said we should do girl things. I helped you because your stupid boy friends were all too big and dumb to be able to climb up in the attic and get the shells."

"Okay. Okay. You were a big help. What do ya want, a medal?"

"No, I just want you to say girls are just as good at things as boys."

"Okay," he said insincerely.

"No, not okay, say it."

"Girls are just as good as boys at things," Randy mumbled begrudgingly. "You happy now?"

"Yup."

Chapter Eleven

IN THE EVENINGS, RANDY and his friends often hung out in our garage, played rock 'n' roll music, shot baskets, well, tried to shoot baskets, and discussed scientific things. Girls their ages would have nothing to do with any of them, so they entertained themselves by doing and saying stupid things.

The evening was a perfect time to open the shells and take out the gunpowder. My parents were tired and never came out to bother them, so they could pretty much do whatever they wanted. We all assembled the next Saturday evening in the garage, ripped open the shotgun cartridges, separated out the BBs, and poured the gunpowder into a pile. Nine boxes of shotgun shells produced quite a pile of gunpowder, which Randy put in an old coffee can that he'd hide in his bedroom until they could decide the launch date. We were careful to put the remainder of the shell casings and the buckshot in a paper bag, which we placed two doors away in a neighbor's trashcan on Sunday night, the night before the city picked up our trashcans.

Monday morning came as it always did, meaning we were supposed to go back to school and our usual routines. Only that Monday started out very differently. At six-thirty a.m., Mom woke us up, telling us to hurry up, get dressed, and go to breakfast. It wasn't what she was telling us to do that sounded strange, but the tone of her voice was tenser than I'd ever heard before. She sounded very nervous. I finished dressing and opened my blinds just as my brother came running out of his room.

"There are cops everywhere!" he said excitedly. "Something big must've happened!"

"What? What do ya mean, big?"

"You know, like an armed robbery or murder or something," he said, both of us now running towards the windows in the front of our house.

"You two get away from those windows right now!" said my mother. "I have no idea what's going on, but I'm calling Mrs. Bixler next door to find out. You two stay completely away from the windows and go eat breakfast. Do you read me?" she said tersely. "I don't want you anywhere near those windows until I find out what's going on. It could be very dangerous. Something serious must be going on to have all those police officers respond at one time, so just go and eat breakfast."

It's difficult to get excited about cold cereal when there are dozens of squad cars parked every which way outside your house, responding to some obviously heinous criminal act.

"Bet someone was murdered last night," said Randy.

"Who would murder someone in this neighborhood?" I asked, alarmed.

"Could be anyone," he said casually.

"What do ya mean, anyone?" I said with more alarm. "Who would do that? No one murders anyone here on our street. Who would Mrs. Bixler murder, Manny the monkey? Who would the Kurths murder, or the Garbers murder? You need to shut up. No one got murdered," I replied trying not to sound panicked. "I'm tellin' Mom what you said."

Mother is now talking with Mrs. Bixler. "Really? Oh, my word...what can that mean?" I heard her saying, my cereal now uneaten and soggy. "Did they say that? Really? That's frightening...and right here in our very own quiet neighborhood," she continued softly. "Yes, my doors are locked. Make sure yours are too, Mrs. Bixler. Yes, we'll call each other if we hear any more. Take care. Yes, you too," she said, hanging up the receiver.

"Well?" my brother and I cried out in unison. "What's happening?"

"Mrs. Bixler says the police have discovered some criminal activity on this street and until they can determine what exactly is going on, the whole neighborhood is on lockdown."

"Lockdown. What does that mean?" asked my brother, unable to hide his excitement.

"Well, apparently, until they find out exactly what's going on and who's involved, no one can leave their homes," said my mom with her usual exaggerated seriousness at the magnitude of just such a situation. "This is nothing to take lightly, children, there's been some kind of serious criminal activity right here in our neighborhood that, for everyone's safety, the police felt it necessary to investigate thoroughly."

"Yeah! No school today," I exclaimed.

"We get to stay home and watch the action," shouted Randy. "How great is that? I'm callin' Duncan to see if he's also on lockdown." He raced to the phone, and I heard him saying, "Yeah, cops everywhere.

Someone was probably murdered or something! Yeah, I know, how cool, huh? Are they by your house, too? No? Wow, I wonder why they're not at your house too. You're only eight houses away. Your mom told you it was just at our end of the block. Wow, that's weird…Yeah, no school today for us. I'll call you later and fill you in. Get my homework assignments, okay?"

"I'm calling Katy too." I grabbed the phone. "Guess what, there're cops everywhere. Yeah, nobody knows what's going on. We're on lockdown at our house, so no school today. Neat, huh? Later."

The excitement of the morning quickly turned into the boredom of a day stuck in the house. Mrs. Bixler did call back and tell our mom that the lockdown had something to do with the garbage collection, but she didn't know much else. Even sneaking peeks out the living room windows to see what was going on when Mom wasn't looking eventually got boring. How many times can you look at police cars parked in front of your house, but not know what was happening?

Randy and I became increasingly bored as the day wore on and resorted to our usual form of entertainment—pushing, shoving, and arguing—eventually getting sent to our rooms for an hour to 'simmer down,' as our folks called it. While in our rooms, there was a loud knock at the front door. We could hear Mom answer it, and a man's voice announced he was a police officer and wanted to come in and ask some questions. My mom invited him in and they sat down in the living room for the questioning.

"Let me first say, we think everyone here on Whitewood Avenue is safe now, so I don't want you to worry. But I have to ask if you've noticed any thing out of the ordinary here in the neighborhood recently, Mrs. Webb?" asked the policeman.

"What do you mean by out of the ordinary, Officer? I'm still unclear on why the police are here. Was someone hurt or something? A burglary perhaps at one of our neighbors' homes?"

"No, nothing like that, ma'am. It's just that your trashman noticed some, well, shall I just say, worrisome items in your neighbor's trashcan."

"Worrisome, Officer? What do you mean by worrisome? Please, tell me what's going on. I have two young children and frankly, I'm worried sick for their safety."

"Well, ma'am, I don't think you have to worry about their safety. It's just that the trashman found a paper bag full of empty shotgun shell casings in your neighbor's trashcan this morning, which concerned him, and he called us so we could investigate."

"Oh my goodness. Empty shell casings? Why in the world would someone put those in a trashcan? That just scares me terribly." Mom wrapped her arms around herself for comfort and shook her head. "Should I be worried about criminals roaming our neighborhood? Is this some new element that may be moving in and threatening our safety and the welfare of our children? I just don't know what to think," she said, her voice trailing off. "Shotgun shell casings? What next?"

"Ma'am, so far we have no evidence any criminal element has moved into your neighborhood. Please don't over react. Our department feels that it was a one-time incident, hopefully with no criminal intent, though we're checking the paper bag at our lab for fingerprints as we speak. I'll get back to you if we find anything that suggests we can identify who the culprit was, all right?"

"Thank you, Officer. Please call me if you find out anything about the person who did this."

"I will, I promise, ma'am." And with that, the police officer left.

I don't know about Randy, but I heard every word the officer said about empty shotgun shell casings found in the neighbor's trashcan in a paper bag and I was on the verge of having a seizure. The part about the police lab checking the paper bag for fingerprints elevated my impending seizure into the massive pediatric stroke category. I stuck my head out of my room and looked towards Randy's room. There he was, hanging outside his door looking down the hall at me with the same panicked look. Shotgun shell casings, criminals, paper bag, police lab for fingerprints. Now what were we going to do?

At dinner, my mom filled all of us in on the day's events and what the police officer had said. My dad was surprised, while Randy and I were unusually quiet. All I could hear banging around in my head was the police lab was checking the paper bag for fingerprints and I knew we'd all touched that bag multiple times before we dumped it in the trashcan. How could we not get caught? Who thought that dumb idea up, and why had we wanted to be a part of Randy's stupid rocket idea anyways? Boys are so dumb!

I was taught to always say prayers before bed, and that night, it seemed particularly important. Mustering all my guilt and remorse, I silently prayed with hands clasped tightly.

Dear God, this is Susan, Susan Webb, you know, the one on Whitewood Avenue in California. I swear I'm done being bad and forgive me for listening to Randy and for getting involved with him and his friends' evil deeds. If you get me out of this mess, I will never do another bad thing ever again. I really mean it. I'm done. Please don't let them find my fingerprints on that paper bag. I know I never should have helped get Dad's shells out of the attic. It was totally Randy's fault that we did it. I'll never again help Randy and his stupid friends make gunpowder for rockets. I promise. Amen.

Not one of the kids involved dared say a word to anyone, including each other, about what had happened. If the topic came up anywhere, we just quietly made eye contact, never admitting we knew anything about the bag or the empty shells. Acknowledgement on any level was too risky and we were all too scared we'd get caught.

The newspaper interviewed the trashman for an article and he bragged he'd saved the town from certain tragedy by finding the bag and calling the police to investigate. According to the Independent Press Telegram a few days later, the lab couldn't identify any of the fingerprints on the paper bag. There was all kinds of speculation as to who might have done it and why someone needed gunpowder, but soon, the interest in the story waned, and the town's focus turned towards the arguments pro and con about new parking meters being installed near the junior college.

After a few weeks, all of us involved felt like we had literally dodged a bullet and we began to relax, though talk about firing the rocket remained taboo. It was too risky to say anything still and we all agreed to put the idea of a launch on hold indefinitely.

Chapter Twelve

ABOUT THREE MONTHS LATER, we were sitting around on our back steps, bouncing Silly Putty as high as we could make it soar when talk returned to missiles and rockets.

"Too bad you can't bounce a missile into the sky with a Silly Putty-like base," said Craig.

"Wouldn't work," answered Charles. "The bounce would break up the fuselage and break off the wings."

"Duh," replied Randy. "Of course it wouldn't work, you stooge. You need to have firepower to launch something into space." With that statement, everyone's collective minds went directly to our rocket still hidden in Randy's room along with the coffee can of gunpowder.

"It's still there in my room, you know." Randy's voice trailed off. "Probably still too risky, don't ya think?"

"Ya, too risky. Bad idea. Too soon. We'll get caught," the group murmured.

"I want no part of it. I promised God I wouldn't do any more bad things. Count me out."

"You do bad things all the time!" said my brother.

"Do not!"

"Do too!"

"Name one," I demanded.

Randy thought for a moment then he motioned for me to come close and whispered in my ear, "I know what you do in the hall at night when Mom and Dad are watching television, so don't tell me you don't do bad things. You better help us or I swear I'll tell Mom on you." He shoved me backwards and laughed. I was aghast at the thought of him knowing what I had done in the hall at night and horror-struck at the thought of him telling my mom, unclear as to which was worse.

"I say we do it soon," said my brother, glancing sideways at me. "Everyone's in, right?"

"Right," everyone murmured hesitantly.

Hell yes, I'm in! Are you kidding me? Not knowing which was worse—my brother knowing what I did buck naked in the hallway at night while my parents are on the other side of the wall watching TV or that he might tell. I'm not only in, but I'll light the dang fuse!

"Let's do it," I stated confidently. "You're in too, Katy, right?"

"Right," she said with little enthusiasm.

We finally agreed the launch would take place the next week, after school, at our garage. Thursday would be the best day, since my mom always visited her mom, took her out to lunch, and went grocery shopping, not returning home until about five-thirty in the evening. If we all hurried, we could rush home from school, change clothes, and reassemble in our garage by three-thirty, leaving us two whole hours to make the launch go as planned before my mom arrived back at the house to start dinner.

To say they actually launched their rocket would be an exaggeration. The boys set up the launch pad on the cement between our kitchen door and the garage, facing west. The idea was to aim the rocket up and slightly over the garage. Their hope was it would ascend, then descend, floating back down using its parachute and landing somewhere in either our backyard, or at worst, in one of our neighbor's backyards.

They loaded the rocket's fuel tank and launching mechanism with gunpowder and attached the fuse. I got the bright idea of getting the four gas masks out of the Webb's Emergency Bomb Bag just to add some drama to the launch. Boner, Charles, Katy, and I put on the masks and we looked like a small heard of elephants with dangling trunks standing around the launch pad. Craig was laughing so hard, he agreed to put one on too.

My brother got mad because we were making a joke out of this serious event, so he and the Mute grabbed the matches and quickly lit the fuse. The fuse sputtered and went out.

"Aw," moaned the herd. "Again! Again! Again!" we yelled indistinguishably from inside the gas masks, our rubber trunks waving from side to side.

Craig ripped off his mask and shouted, "Come on, light it!" Randy relit the fuse and the flame moved towards the launch pad slowly then quicker and then...nothing happened.

"What the..." my brother said under his breath. "Charles, what's wrong with the fuse?"

"I dunno," he said, fumbling with his gas mask.

"Well, fix it, for Christ's sake! We're running out of time!"

"Yeah...yeah...give me a sec," said Charles, staring at the pad, looking puzzled. "Okay! I got it! The red and blue wires are backwards. Move outta the way." With that, he switched the wires and lit the fuse again.

There was a lot of smoke, aroma of hot gunpowder, and then with a bang, the rocket lifted off and smashed into the corner of our garage with a flurry of sparks and fire. The rocket maybe a traveled a total of six feet in altitude.

"Ah shit!" we all said in unison.

Our wooden roof shingles were on fire, and the rocket, engulfed in flames, was on the cement below. Flames quickly began to spread to the inside of the garage. Gas masks still in place, Katy and I ran for the garden hose like firefighters springing into action. While we aimed the hose at the roof, Randy and the Mute tried to stamp out the flames inside the garage with their shoes and a towel. Charles was on his toes, flapping his arms as if trying to fly out of the frightening scene.

Our next-door neighbor, Mrs. Bixler, came out of her house, saw the smoke, and began shouting, "Fire! Fire!" Manny was now hootin' and howlin' excitedly from his cage like a soundtrack from Tarzan the Ape Man.

"Get on the horn and call the fire department!" My brother shouted back to Mrs. Bixler. Katy and I continued battling the rising flames on the roof as the water ran off its pitch in a steady, steamy stream. We heard the sirens wailing towards our house getting closer, though by now Randy and the Mute had pretty well knocked down the flames inside the garage. Bobby had taken off his gas mask and was pivoting around in a circle trying to decide what, if anything, he should do.

"Take the hose!" I instructed him. "Just keep aiming the water towards the roof. Katy will help you. Just go! Go!"

My focus shifted from the roof on fire to the fact our mom should be arriving home at any moment to a horrible mess. There was water, and charred wood roof shingles everywhere, along with a lot of soot and ash. The fire department arrived and finished off the fire. Then they took all of us out to the front yard and lined us up along the fire truck to get our version of what had just happened. Craig, Bobby, Katy, and I were in the lineup, still clutching our elephant-like gas masks. My brother's face was ashen under the smeared soot. Charles was stammering and flapping, and Duncan was mute as always. Then up drove our seafoam green Galaxy 500.

In my mother's line of vision, there were seven children, two of them particularly familiar, four clutching gas masks, and a fire official, who was interviewing the children. All the while, a monkey was screeching in the background, and a local newspaper reporter was taking notes. A fire hose was running from the truck, up the driveway, and into her backyard. Water was everywhere. There were eight city firefighters and a large group of neighbors all talking and gesturing towards her garage and backyard. So much was going on, I didn't see my mom arrive. The corner of the garage and some of the roof was burned. Everyone's parents were immediately called and there was a four-family meeting. (Granny Bonner was too drunk to attend, Bobby's mom was still at work, and Duncan was raised by wolves.)

The newspaper reporter wanted to interview all seven of us kids, but our parents agreed unanimously that was a bad idea, as it would make us feel like celebrities rather than the true felons we actually were. Our house and street just seemed to be some kind of magnet for exciting newsworthy events, the reporter had commented, much to my mother's embarrassment.

We all were put on restriction for a month and had to do additional chores and pay restitution. Our family's fire insurance covered some of the fire damage, but not all, since it wasn't an act of nature nor of God, nor an accident, just seven idiot kids.

My brother actually got in more trouble than I did, which was unusual, but since it appeared the accident involved a rocket, he must have played a greater role in the whole mess. I dramatically, and without remorse, reassured my parents it was his entire fault because it involved rockets and explosives, of which were of no interest to me.

The end of this disaster was not quite in sight, however. To top off the whole ugly event, our dog, Queenie, bit the contractor who came to repair the garage roof, and the Health Department placed her on quarantine for four weeks in case the man contracted rabies. He tried to sue my parents; however, we did have a sign on the gate that said, "Beware of Dog," which he ignored, so in the end it was his own fault. Queenie, Randy, and I were released on parole the same Friday, one month to the day after the 'Great Garage Fire on Whitewood Avenue,' as the local newspaper reported it.

Chapter Thirteen

IN THE BEGINNING OF sixth grade, my mom insisted I begin to grow my hair out, and though it didn't seem like it at the time, it was the end of feeling I had any control over either my body or my life, for the next three years. In some crazy kind of mother-wisdom, she knew I needed to have longer hair to fit into junior high school. Misguided though much of her help usually ended up being, she was right; you couldn't go into seventh grade with a ducktail and survive.

Sixth grade was my final year enrolled in Don's and Deb's. I had gone through a myriad of dresses and shoes, hating each and every outfit and the class itself. This year, the instructors hinted, would be different and much better than the last four years. This year was going to focus on real teenage dance styles, the instructors told us excitedly. The Twist, the Mashed Potatoes, the Pony, the Watusi, and the Swim, dances that kids were actually doing. All the girls were so excited. The boys and I were not. Who needed to know these dances? No one danced; it was stupid. Guys don't actually dance, nor am I gonna dance. Who'd I dance with anyway? Willy the midget?

By now, some of the boys and girls were actually couples and going steady with each other. Sherryl and Kenny had exchanged some vow of love, as had Ralph and Debby, though I heard he had to go throw up first because he was so nervous about asking her. Ralph going steady with a girl. Who'd have ever thought that would happen? To show her sincerity, Debby baked Ralph a dozen pecan cookies. Heck, I would have said yes to Debby to get a dozen of her homemade pecan cookies. Even though parents tried to discourage their kids from becoming couples at this age, the reality was we were heading for junior high school and that's what teenagers did.

The summer before seventh grade, Katy and I spent hours on weekends at the empty campus of Long Beach City College. We'd graduated from smoking dry daylily stems on the side of my parent's house to smoking real cigarette butts lit with the matches we found on the campus. We hung out there with all the other neighborhood kids who were finishing elementary school, smoking, teasing, bragging, and acting out. It was beginning to dawn on me that Katy and the other girls were becoming much more interested in talking about boys, clothes, and makeup, while I was still more attracted to sports and tools.

It wasn't like one day we were skateboarding and riding bikes and the next day they were wearing makeup. But still, things were changing between all of us and I could sense we were heading in different directions. Rory had already stopped hanging out with us, upon his older sister's insistence it would damage his reputation as he was already in junior high school. My heart hurt from his absence, and my life was beginning to go from great to not so great.

"What are you looking forward to most in junior high school?" asked Katy one day while we were laying in the grass at the college.

"I don't really know. I'm not sure what to expect," I said thoughtfully.

"My sister says the boys get cuter and the homework harder."

"Neither one of those things sounds particularly good to me. I hate homework and I'm not interested in having a boyfriend, so it doesn't look like there's much to look forward to. You're lucky 'cause you get to go to school with Rory. Nobody we hang out with is going to my school. I'm not looking forward to making all new friends."

"It's gonna be weird not seeing you almost every day," said Katy.

"Yeah, really weird, but I guess it'll all work out," I said, feeling sad at that reality.

"We'll catch back up again in high school," answered Katy encouragingly.

"Yeah...for sure, in high school," was my reply though not feeling particularly encouraged by how far away that sounded.

***

My mother's recollection was that I started crying the first day of seventh grade and didn't stop crying until starting high school. That's perhaps an exaggeration, but not a great one. After Katy went to the other junior high school, the loss of her support and companionship made my life much more stressful. She'd been my friend, my buddy, and my accomplice. She'd always run a form of Social Appropriateness 101 for me when I was clueless as to what was normal and helped me fit in when I wouldn't have on my own.

Katy and Rory lived one block west of our street and out of my school's boundaries, so they went to Hoover Junior High School. Rory had already been at Hoover the previous year and was now comfortably in eighth grade, playing on their baseball team. Katy immediately became the most popular seventh grade girl and was asked to be on the school's pep squad, so she easily fit in too. They were Hoover Junior High School Hawks—The Mighty Hawks.

The street where we lived had Bancroft Junior High School as the home school. Leaving sixth grade confident and secure in my rank within my peers, I entered junior high thinking that status would remain the same. I was so wrong. Now that I was on my own, without my best friends, I had no idea of how bad things were going to get. To make everything worse, our new junior high school's mascot was a beaver. So what's the big deal? Not quite what I'd imagined when listening to the Beach Boys, Be True to Your School. A damn beaver. Now totally alone and a Bancroft Beaver. How fierce was a beaver? Who would a beaver impress? They built damns, for God's sake. Oh, look out for the scary beaver.

Everyone who didn't attend Bancroft called us the Damn Beavers, and all kids knew a 'beaver' was a slang word for a girl's crotch. If your legs weren't appropriately and tightly crossed, you'd be 'shootin' a beaver.' Who'd want their school mascot to be a nasty crotch word? Every other junior high school in Long Beach had a mascot like a lion, a falcon, or at least a husky, but no, at Bancroft, we were the Damn Beavers. Just more potential for ridicule, in my mind.

The unspoken rules of junior high school propelled many of us new seventh graders into situations where we were totally incapable of functioning. There were the 'rules,' which I was not familiar with, and there were the 'superstitions and traditions' of which I had no knowledge.

These social guidelines were particularly difficult for those who didn't have older brothers and sisters to pass down the wisdom, knowledge, superstitions, and rituals. But wait, you say, what about Randy? He was older so didn't he learn the rules and pass the knowledge down? The short answer was no. The long answer was, "hell, no!" He didn't pass down one iota of the coveted junior high school traditions or knowledge to his little sister. Nope, he flat-ass hung her out to dry.

On the first day of school, I realized my utter cluelessness as to what was deemed acceptable or not acceptable. Adding more confusion to my already increasingly murky social awareness was that many of the things one could or could not do socially was based on gender roles.

For example, I quickly found out girls carried their books and folders in their arm, elbow bent, up against their breasts, assuming that you had them. Boys carried their books in their hand, down to their side. If even for a second you had your books in your hand down by your side, eyebrows were raised, snickers could be heard, and your sexual orientation was swiftly questioned.

There were two more tests at Bancroft Junior High that determined to everyone in the student body what sex you actually were. One of the tests that indicated questionable sex-orientation was the writing test. If you placed your paper in front of you facing up and down or tilted it back towards your left, you obviously had male dominated tendencies. For every left-handed girl or girl who wrote slightly backhanded like I did, the future was doomed. Real girls' handwriting slanted to the right; everyone knew that.

The last test was clearly the most conclusive. If you were asked to look at your fingernails and you placed your hands out in front of you with fingers splayed, you should have been a boy. Girls only checked their nails by closing their hands and turning their nails towards them as if checking your polish.

By Wednesday of the first week of school, I had failed all three sex-determination tests. It was clear to me, based on the results of these irrefutable scientific tests, I should've been born a boy. Later that evening, alone in my room, I tried unsuccessfully to kiss my elbow one more time.

Still, there was more humiliation to endure for us uninformed. Girls who wore red on Thursdays were whores. All seventh grade students around the globe, including the small soviet nation known as Krabeckastan, apparently knew this fact well. However, for the unenlightened few like me, the news regarding wearing the color red on Thursdays came one critical day too late.

"You look really nice in red," said my mother on Thursday of the first week of school. "You should wear that red blouse to school today."

"Yeah, okay," said the innocent lamb, unknowingly being led to the slaughter. "Baa! Baa!"

"You look so nice today," said the smiling leader of teenage genocide as I left for school.

That Thursday morning, I met my friend at the corner of her block so we could walk the rest of the way to school as we had prearranged the night before on the phone. The closer I got to the corner, the more horrified I could tell she looked.

"What are you doing?" she said in a monotone as I approached.

"What are you talking about?" annoyed at the question so early in the morning. At least let me get to school before the pressure and questions start.

"Why are you wearing red today? It's Thursday."

"Yeah," pretending to be cool and bobbing my head, "So?"

"Don't you know about wearing the color red on Thursdays? It means you're a whore!" She said as if I must have suffered a recent head injury that robbed me of my sanity.

"What?" I replied with concern.

"Yeah. How could you not know that? Everyone knows if you wear red on Thursdays you're a whore," she said with attitude, and emphasis on the word 'everyone.'

"Oh my God," breaking into a sweat at seven-thirty a.m. when the temperature was barely sixty-five degrees. The following thoughts ran through my mind like a Super-8 projector on fast forward. Should I go home and change, borrow something to cover it up, run away, or just kill myself?

Approaching the school, the buzzing sound of the first period warning bell interrupted my frantic thoughts. My fate was sealed and I would forever be known as a Bancroft Junior High School whore from this day on, marked with a big red 'W' on my forehead.

"Here," she said, stripping off her sweater, "put this on and button it up. You owe me big time." I took her sweater, quickly buttoned it up to cover my red blouse, and we headed for homeroom. Holy Mother of God, get me through the rest of this already crappy day, I prayed.

Problems caused by my lack of knowledge regarding important social rules were second only to problems created by my height. In elementary school, being tall wasn't much of an issue. Adults commented on my height frequently, but kids who I'd grown up with didn't seem to take much notice. In seventh grade, I became intensely aware of my constantly increasing height, forever reminded of it whether shopping for clothes that never fit in the arms or legs, listening to the Jolly Green Giant commercial on TV, or being teased by kids at school. There was no denying it; I was unusually tall.

Every August, my mother would take me to buy new clothes and shoes for the fall. By fifth grade, no longer able to fit in the clothes in the children's section, and there was no teen section in those days, I was forced to shop in the women's department. Mom would either try to alter all my clothes to fit or sew me new ones because a child dressed in women's clothing never looked cute or stylish, only awkward. In fifth and sixth grade, how my school clothes looked wasn't so important to me, but now in junior high school, it was important to me to look like every other girl in my school.

So even though my mom was an excellent seamstress, there's only so much that can be done to make a woman's dress look anything like what a seventh grade girl would choose to wear in 1963. Since eventually I couldn't fit in clothes available in stores at all, she began to make all of my school and church clothes.

My mother would drag me to fabric stores to look at McCall clothes patterns, embarrassingly measure me numerous times right there in the store with a measuring tape she always kept in her purse, then buy a foot more material than the pattern requested while politely disagreeing with the fabric store staff as to the necessary additional yardage. Once home, she'd furiously get on to the task of sewing my entire wardrobe of new school clothes. For the most part, I had the same accordion skirts, blouses, and jackets the girls in junior high were wearing, except my own personal seamstress was making them—and I hated it. It was one more way to make me feel different from all the other girls in junior high, and a few times my mother's home tailoring occasionally caused me to get flat out busted.

"Where did you get that color blouse?" asked a girl at school.

"At MayCo," I replied casually.

"In what department?"

"I forget," I said, still trying to sound casual.

"I was just there shopping over the weekend and I didn't see any blouses that color. The salesgirl said they'd just received a new shipment, too."

"This color was probably sold out already."

"Are you sure you got it at MayCo?"

"Yup, I'm sure."

"I'll look again, but I swear there were none that color."

"Good idea." Making a mental note to be more specific in the future with color details to my private seamstress.

I haven't mentioned the fact that, going into junior high school, I wore a size eight shoe. Who wore size eight? Only my mother and a few other fifty-year-old women. Who wanted to wear the type of shoes they wore? No seventh grader.

Searching for appropriate shoes for a girl who wore a size eight at the start of junior high school was about as promising as mining for diamonds in your backyard. If we could even find size eight shoes, they were usually some type of orthopedic shoe that looked like you also should probably be using crutches for mobility, and definitely not suited for a seventh grade girl. Usually only Keds tennis shoes were in my size, and few, if any girls but me, wore them to school.

Each September, the nurse would call every student enrolled at Bancroft to her office, where she'd weigh us, measure us, and make sure we were up to date on all of our immunizations. This event began in first grade and continued through high school. Once in junior high school, this ritual regrettably took place in the hall outside the nurse's office so there was no shelter from public humiliation.

For anyone tall, short, or fat, this ordeal was definitely cruel and unusual punishment. The majority of students were in the average category, in the proverbial bell-shaped curve. However, for those of us who fell outside, especially way outside the norm, we could only describe the thought of being weighed and measured in front of a line of your peers as humiliating.

Our junior high school nurse called dozens of kids in alphabetical order to her office at the same time. We formed a long line in the hall where she'd temporarily placed her Health-O-Meter Professional Beam Scale with a metal height-rod. This meant I stood waiting in line with all the kids whose last name started with "W," like Wagoner, Winslow, and the twins William and Wesley Woodle. When the nurse would call my name, I'd try to slump shorter by compressing the bones in my neck. But when the nurse would hoist the metal height rod up from the top of the scale, each year I was inevitably taller—inches taller—than the previous year.

"Susan Webb," the nurse shouted to her assistant, who documented the information on your permanent school record, "is sixty-six inches tall," she'd continue, "one of our tallest students, and she weighs in at one hundred and twenty pounds."

I felt like a heavy weight boxer checking in for her next match. As bad as it was for me, I felt more sympathy for Wesley and William Woodle, the fat, identical twins whose mother dressed them in the same awful matching outfits. Kids were even meaner to them than they were to some of us other misfits. Dressed daily in identical clothing, they wore large matching madras or striped shirts, and black slacks with black hard leather shoes. The striped shirts made them look like circus tents and the madras ones like huge, plaid weather balloons. When their turn came to get on the scale, the line would erupt in comments.

"They'll break the scale!"

"It's not meant for elephants!"

"Step right up! Oh look, it's Porky and Dorky, the Waddling twins!"

"Look out, they'll sit on you!"

Or more insulting, "The scale doesn't go that high in pounds!"

Elephant trumpeting sounds echoed down the hallway. "Watch out, they may stampede!"

The nurse's assistant sat at a nearby table, trying to shush the kids in line, while taking notes and documenting the latest information announced loudly by the nurse.

Once William, with tears in his eyes, confided in me that he hated every September when he had to be weighed. He told me he started worrying about being measured and weighed in August, and it ruined the whole end of the summer vacation. He confessed that before getting on the scale, he'd go pee, and then when he got up on the scale he'd let out all of the air in his lungs in hopes of losing a few pounds between the air and the pee. I told him the kids who teased him were just idiots and to ignore them, and his mom was probably right—he and his brother were just big boned.

"That's easy for you to say," said William sadly, "'cause you're kinda normal."

"What are you talking about, William? Kinda normal? I'm a giant, if you haven't noticed. Are all those striped and plaid shirts blinding you?" I asked, shaking my head with annoyance.

"No, I know you're tall, Susan, but at least you're not fat!" said William seriously.

"What the hell does it matter, William? Fat, short, tall, or whatever? Not fitting in stinks no matter why you don't fit in." I was now shouting at him.

"I'm sorry...I just would rather be too tall than too fat," he said quietly.

"You can stop eating, you moron. I can't stop growing. If I could, don't ya think I would? I hate being tall," I said seething with anger, and afraid of crying. "I'm sick of being made fun of because I'm so tall and I hate not fitting in!" The volume of my voice served to quiet everyone in line, so I stomped back down the hall to my math class in total silence.

After we were measured at the beginning of seventh grade, I secretly started to measure my own growth at home in my bedroom. With my bedroom door closed, I'd stand with my back to the door, place a pencil on the top of my head, and make a mark. Then, with my twelve-inch ruler, measure from the ground to the mark and write the number in really tiny numbers, putting the calendar back up on the back of my bedroom door so it hid my measurements.

The first time, my height was five-feet-six and a half inches tall. The next time, months later, I had grown two more inches and had to move the nail up on the door that held the calendar to cover the new mark. It was so depressing, because no matter how much slouching or trying to will my neck bones to compress, I continued to grow.

Unable to stop or even slow down this process, I secretly declared to myself if I grew over five-feet-eleven-inches, I'd commit suicide. To make sure my body understood the seriousness of the threat, I measured five feet-eleven inches and made a red line on the back of my bedroom door with a marker. There, that means business. Go over this line and it's over.

In my own naïve way, I thought if I threatened my body, I might gain control over it and then over its ability to grow. I actually thought I could stop my height at five-feet-eleven-inches, though in my mind, I'd still be unusually tall, but at least not six feet tall. Only men were six feet tall, not women.

In my never-ending hope of fitting in, I begrudgingly went steady with big, dumb Jack Mott, whose family was rumored to be members of the Italian mafia. Not the pretend mafia, but the real Sicilian mafia. In seventh grade, going steady meant you weren't supposed to be interested in any other boy but the one you were going with. That was easy for me. I didn't like boys, and I didn't like Jack, but it served, ever so slightly, to make me feel normal, so I played along and wore Jack's turquoise-blue St. Christopher. Looking back at it, St. Christopher being de-sainted was probably an omen for me. He wasn't going to remain a saint and I wasn't going to remain heterosexual.

However, for a brief moment, pretending to be a typical seventh grade girl, going steady with a tall, sweaty Sicilian boy with jet-black hair and blue eyes, who kept snapping the back of my bra every time he walked up behind me, seemed to be a small price to pay for feeling accepted.

With each snap of my bra, it took all of my inner strength to keep from knocking him upside the head, remembering my mother's words, "That wouldn't be lady-like, Susan." Our relationship lasted about two days before we officially broke up. Within a week, he gave the very same St. Christopher medal to Veronica Hunter. Honestly, they made a much better couple.

Chapter Fourteen

SEVENTH GRADE MEANT MAKEUP, nylons, and ratted or teased hair for most of the other girls at Bancroft Junior High School. For me, it meant no makeup, talcum powder in my shoes, and no rats in my hair. I begged and pleaded, trying to get my mom to understand that by not allowing me to rat and spray my hair, and wear nylons and makeup, she was dooming me to a life in the ranks of the junior high outcastes. What did she know? What did she care? I might as well be a leper.

"Ratting your hair will give you split ends," she'd say. "You should brush your hair one hundred times every night before you go to bed. It distributes your natural oils and makes your hair shiny and healthy." What planet are you from, distributes natural oils? Who the hell cares?

"Talcum powder makes your shoes fit better," she'd state with conviction, as if she'd been a shoe salesman in a prior life. "Good shoes make for good posture." She'd continue to preach. "No one likes a tall girl who slumps or has poor posture," she'd say cheerily. "Be proud of your height, Susan."

Oh, yeah, I'm so happy I'm a giant. Who could ask for more? I'd think.

"Girls who wear nylons have bad reputations," she'd say, as if that too was a universally known fact, "and usually they have pierced ears." That was another object on her disapproval list, which I also wanted but dared not even hope to ever acquire. That also meant they probably had 'loose personal morals,' she'd infer, ending her statement and nodding in agreement with herself. I hated her never-ending string of old-fashioned ideas of what was good, and what was not, and it made my school life a living hell.

"You are not going to do any of these things. Period," declared Mother Moses in her sermon from the mount, bushes burning all around her, as if the rules were now inscribed on some stone tablet, and I felt my life beginning to career even more out of control.

No wonder I cried a lot. Who cared about my split ends and looking like a whore? It would have been an improvement over my current caste as one of the school's untouchables. She had no idea how important these things were to me in hopes of the popular group accepting me. She had no friends and never socialized, and she didn't care about fitting in. Trying to keep my sanity, I frantically thought of ways to get around her rules.

A few of the girls from school who also had strict mothers would take their makeup and nylons to school in their purse and put them on in the restroom before homeroom. The problem was having no nylons or makeup to take to school and put on in the bathroom, hall, closet, or any other place. They all had older sisters, but I only had Randy and as far as I knew, he hadn't gotten into wearing nylons and makeup. It was time to do something, so I took my money and secretly bought a package of nylons at the corner Woolworths. My thinking was if I just had the nylons, I too could secretly put them on in the girl's bathroom before first period.

The problem was at twelve, I was already over five-feet-six inches tall. In those days, they didn't have tall sizes in anything, especially in nylons, so I was forced to get the regular size, and hope for the best. After looking through all of my choices of colors of nylons, the package labeled Suntan seemed the best choice because the description on the back of the package said if you wore this brand you'd look like 'you'd been sunbathing all summer and were kissed by the sun.' To have been kissed by the summer sun sounded great to me, since nothing had ever kissed me.

As I took the nylons out of the package, two things became clear. Compared to my skin tone, 'kissed by the summer sun' looked like my legs had suddenly turned the color of mahogany, while the rest of my body was pasty white. More alarming, you needed something to hold the nylons in place. I just assumed they came with some device that made them stay and not fall down around your ankles. My only solution was to use rubber bands. The directions said attach the nylons to your garter belt, which was an unknown entity to me. What was it? Where did it come from? How did it hold the nylons up? Rubber bands were the extent of my limited knowledge, and it was quickly apparent, rubber bands weren't going to hold these reddish-brown nylons anywhere.

The next crisis was the top of the nylons barely came above my knee, even if I stretched them to their limit. In addition, with every step, the nylons slid down my legs towards my ankles. All of the other girls' nylons were above thigh high and on the shorter girls, almost up to their underpants. These girls were of average size, at five to five-feet-three-inches, while I was in the 'pushing five-feet-seven inches' club. Frustrated, I just shoved the nylons into my t-shirt drawer.

Why me? All my missing information on nylons and garters, along with my mother's insistence that I had to dust talcum powder into my shoes, just added to my sense of being a total loser. It was unbelievable to me that the previous year in sixth grade, I'd been at the top of the social status ladder. Now I was close to the bottom rung and it was a miserable feeling. No nylons, no makeup, not one ratted hair on my head, but by God, my size eight Keds shoes fit well with talcum powder.

I think my constant stream of tears made my mom afraid her child was approaching a diagnosis of clinical depression or possible suicide. After one siege of uncontrollable sobbing, she relented and gave me money to buy one pair of nylons and gave me one of her own garter belts. Nylons are expensive, she cautioned, you have to take care of them.

"One pair should last you at least one month," she stated with motherly wisdom. "Also, remember the color of the nylons should match your skin tone, so hold them up against your arm to make sure they match."

With this said, I was given formal permission to be released from the lowest caste of girls in school and rise to the next level of junior high purgatory. I was elated, and immediately off to Woolworth's on my bike to purchase my first legitimate pair of nylons. For once, everything now seemed hopeful.

Slowly thumbing through the packages of nylons, checking each color, their descriptions rolled through my mind. Summer Sunrise—too dark, Summer Breeze—still way too dark, as I compared it to the color on my right forearm. How about the Lightly Kissed package—dang, still much darker than my arm. Coming across the last package in the bin called Natural Nursing Neutral, I held it up against my arm. It's pretty close, except wait, the definition read, 'Perfect to be worn with your white nursing dress and hat, while covering any blemishes on your legs.' What the hell, my white nurse's dress? Jeez. I grabbed the Lightly Kissed package and headed for the cash register. My skin color is Natural Nursing Neutral? How can that be?

Racing home and into my room, I put on the garter belt, then sat on the edge of my bed and attempted to attach the nylons to the garters, just like I watched the other girls do in the bathroom. Noticing how difficult it was to stretch and attach the garter to the nylons, I found if you let go before attaching it stably, the metal part snapped backwards, stinging whatever part of your body it hit. Worse yet, the three-inch piece of elastic that held each fastener stretching a maximum of two inches on most girls, needed more like twelve inches of stretch on my frame.

In order for the garter belt to be long enough to get from the belt down to the top of the nylon, each garter had to stretch to its absolute maximum capacity. To make matters worse, when I finally stood up, the garter belt was pulled down way below my pubic bone and the nylons remained just barely above my knees. The only way this was going to work was if I hunched over as I walked. Unfortunately, this would practically require me to walk in a sitting position.

My mother kept knocking on my bedroom door, asking, "How is it going?" and I'd reply cheerily, "Great." But it was evident this was not going great.

Finally showing her the problem; she took my nylons to the kitchen and wet them. In a moment, she returned with four cans of Campbell's Chicken Soup, slipping two cans into each nylon, then she tied the nylons to clothes hangers, and hung the hanger up on the top of the doorjamb of my room. To my amazement, the nylons slowly stretched and gained a few inches. I was now hopeful the nylons would at least now be higher than my knees; which in my situation, any additional inches were small miracles. This was one of the first times I felt like my mom might actually be on my side—as if she was almost a friend. But that feeling was short lived.

"Did you put talcum powder in your shoes?" she asked the next morning.

"No, I have on nylons."

"You still have to put talcum powder in your shoes to make them fit right," Mom said again.

"Why? No one else has talcum powder in their shoes."

"They just don't have a mother that cares about their feet."

No, I thought, they have mothers who care about peer pressure and acceptance.

"No talcum powder. No nylons," she said as she walked away.

"Okay, okay," was my response, already weary and not wanting the conversation to last a moment longer. Dumping talcum powder in both shoes, I stomped out of the house. The day seemed to be going better than usual, which is relative in the scope of life in junior high school, until I tripped into a locker on the way to homeroom period and punched a hole in my new nylon.

Crap, I needed some nail polish to stop the run, which was beginning to spread as I looked on helplessly. Frantically, I looked for someone I knew in class who might have nail polish, but my friends who wore nail polish were nowhere to be found. Girls who had nail polish in their purses fell into the same category as girls who pierced their ears, in my mother's book of acceptable behaviors, and I knew of frightfully few girls who did either. The bell rang and I walked to my desk, knowing that by sitting down, the run would probably split both upward and downward from the original ding, dooming any chance I could wear the nylons again.

For some miraculous reason the run in my nylons only left a hole at my knee. I felt blessed, as if I'd received a liver transplant at the last moment. My nylons could be saved for future wear. I managed to make it to gym period, where there was time to take off the nylons and safely put them into my notebook folder, so I could deal with the problem later.

Lulled into complacency and feeling like my mom might still be on my side after her recent Campbell's Chicken Soup solution, I arrived home and showed her the hole and she indicated she knew just the answer to my problem.

"I need nail polish to keep them from running any further," I told her, having seen girls stop runs in their nylons at school with fingernail polish dozens of times.

"Only girls who don't have proper supervision use nail polish," my mother replied, meaning again, they were probably prostitutes in the making, if not already practicing their trade.

"What does proper supervision have to do with stopping nylons from running?" not wanting to hear her rant on nail polish, nylons, and pierced ears.

"I'll take care of them," she said, whisking them away.

Oh, great. My mother's 'fixing' the run her way. I just know it will be a wonderful solution. Hoping against all odds she might actually do something to help me for a second time that decade, I went to my room to do my homework, and promptly forgot about my pending problem.

As I got out of bed the next morning with my usual junior high school enthusiasm, annoyance at the world in general, and my life specifically, was my primary focus. Never a morning person, or an evening person, I was more of the middle of the day person, so I was always unhappy at the early hour I was forced to arise.

The limited options of what to wear made my lousy mood worse. I finally found an outfit and while looking around for my nylons, I remembered my mother was going to 'fix them' for me. I trudged to the kitchen and asked where my nylons were and my mom pointed to the counter. I grabbed them and returned to my room to put them on, only to find she had used thick brown-colored darning thread to sew up the hole. She literally darned the hole in my nylons shut, as if they were a pair of old socks.

Already late to school, I put on the nylons, praying silently the web would be above my hem. I checked in the mirror and was relieved to see the run and the entire sewn up area was just above the edge of my skirt.

Off to school I charged, sliding into my chair in homeroom just as the tardy bell rang. I looked down at my skirt and, to my horror, the brown, darned spider web was visible, spreading out on my right knee and continuing under the hem of my skirt. I tried to adjust it, but would have needed an ankle-length prairie skirt to hide that web. Within in a few moments, a homeroom predator noticed my knee and my mother's darning project, and the snickering and pointing began. In junior high school, laughter is contagious; somewhat like the bubonic plague, it quickly touches everyone in its path. The laughter spread until the teacher stopped the class to ask about the problem.

"Susan has a spider web on her leg!" said one girl.

"Maybe she has spiders in her pants and they made webs on her legs!" offered another.

"Or possibly she's a real spider!" added Jerky Jerry Winslow.

Knowing nothing I could do or say would stop the pestering, I just sat frozen, feeling homeroom would never end. Again, vowing to never trust my mother, I threw the nylons away in the bathroom, and I remained bare legged for the rest of the day. Swearing not to consult with her on any future problem with nylons or anything else, I just couldn't risk anymore ridicule or mockery.

I'm such a loser; why wasn't I born a boy? It would have been so much easier. Clothes would have fit, I wouldn't have to wear crappy nylons, and it would've been okay to be good at sports. Life would have been great. But no, I'm this giant girl who can't fit in anywhere. Why me? I gazed down at my elbow.

Chapter Fifteen

GYM CLASS WAS THE one place in my junior high school day I felt positive, happy, and in control. I was always good at physical activity, and I could wear gym clothes instead of skirts, so P.E. became an oasis to just be myself. I loved gym and the gym teachers loved me—usually. For the most part, P.E. gave me a much-needed respite in a teenage world requiring more social knowledge than I had access to. It also allowed me a whole period to torment Carol Laguardia without mercy.

It started the first day of school in gym class. She was flirty and sleazy-looking, with bright red lipstick, dyed black hair, and was an exotic beauty in my eyes. I immediately fell madly in love with her. Just the way she tossed her hair made me giddy. In addition, she was both easy to tease and seemed to enjoy my attention. She and her friend, Sharon, would call my house on their party lines, and we would talk for hours while I teased and flirted with Carol. If my mother had half a clue, she would have picked up on the fact that most girls did not talk to other girls for hours without once mentioning a boy's name. Mom just seemed oblivious to what other 'normal teenage girls' were doing. Another missed clue, just like the preschool teacher's note observing, "Susan only wants to wear her brother's clothes."

As my 'relationship' with Carol grew deeper in my mind, my actions got bolder, waiting for her at lunch, teasing her, grabbing her books, and generally making a total pest of myself. To make matters more difficult, the boys also liked Carol because she was flirty and sleazy, so there was major competition. Unknowingly, we were vying for the same thing—her undivided, catty, flirty attention. Never to be outdone, I constantly tried to think of creative and new ways of getting her to notice me and forget the stupid boys. One day in gym class, my best plan materialized.

Mrs. Priget was known around school as a very strict P.E. teacher who did not like girls that forgot their gym suits or girls who were disruptive in class. I didn't fall into the first category, but definitely fell into the second. Mrs. Priget had already made it clear by her scowl that she didn't appreciate all my comments and antics used to impress my 'girlfriend' Carol.

One day, Mrs. Priget reprimanded me for leading the warm-up exercises in a loud Scottish brogue accent. Carol snickered while Mrs. Priget chided me, and this just hyped me up even more. We were heading back to the locker room when I came across a floppy, dead sparrow lying on the playground. I picked it up and wiggled it in Carol's face; she screamed and stepped back, laughing as she told me to stop. She started to run towards the girl's dressing room with me galloping right behind her, holding the dead, dangling bird by one wing, running through the locker room and into the bathroom. Shrieking, she slammed the stall door, and locked it.

High on adrenaline and lust, I was totally unaware everyone in the girl's locker room began crowding into the small bathroom to see what was causing all the commotion. Carol continued to scream. Her stall was locked and the bathroom was so full of junior high girls Carol couldn't have opened the stall door even if she had wanted. I hung the dead bird over the top and Carol's hysterical screeching crescendo was ear piercing. I'm not sure if it was the screaming or just the mob mentality, but the other girls started pushing and shoving, falling over each other to get out of the bathroom as quickly as possible. Carol continued to howl like a banshee, trapped in the stall by the crowd while I periodically taunted her by dangling the dead bird back over the top of the door.

So engrossed with my own pleasure, I didn't even notice everyone had fled the bathroom. Standing by the sinks, grinning from ear to ear like a fool holding the limp body, I hung the bird over the top of the door of the stall one more time and Carol's shriek rose to a new horror movie intensity, echoing within the lavatory walls. At this instant, in charged Mrs. Priget, trying to determine the exact location of the hysteria. So there I was, holding a dead bird while Carol Laguardia screamed hysterically at the top of her lungs. Mrs. Priget was livid, and demanded we proceed immediately to her office to explain ourselves. Carol went first. I don't know what she told Mrs. Priget, but I'm sure it wasn't my version. My story was I was just trying to show Carol the dead bird we were using as a science project. Mrs. Priget had already contacted my mother by the time I got home from school, with the dreadful details of my behavior.

After conducting her own fact-finding investigation on what I'd done at school and to whom, she said there were to be no more conversations with Carol on the phone. My mom put the kibosh on my first female relationship. I'm sure my mom made a mental note confirming I was methodically heading towards trouble down the road, though she stayed silent. But when my grandmother heard the story, she would have lots to say about the direction her granddaughter was heading.

***

In 1963, President John F. Kennedy announced America's youth were out of shape and unable to compete at a physical fitness level with the other countries of the civilized world. Good nutrition and physical activity were his administration's battle cry to American youth. Thus, began the JFK Physical Fitness campaign to identify the most physically fit student in each junior high school throughout the United States.

We were given information to take home to our parents, outlining how much physical activity we should be getting each day and how our parents could help us to become fit by giving us the right foods to eat. In my house, this was a joke, because my mother probably prepared better meals for us than Mrs. Kennedy and the White House staff prepared for the First Family.

My dad had a good job and we always had milk, salad, and bread and butter with our main course, which was chicken, pork, or often steak. Martha Webb was so concerned with what her family ate that every year she would go to a Dutch butcher, purchase half a cow, have it cut and packaged, and would store it in a huge freezer in our kitchen. Her family was not going to eat store bought meat because it was not fresh. How our frozen meat was fresher never really made sense to me, but no one argued with my mother on her theories. She just knew. I did sometimes wonder who was eating the other half of our cow. Were they in a family like ours that set the nutrition bar high? Did those kids long for hotdogs and bologna like we did?

We weren't allowed to eat hotdogs or hamburgers except on very special occasions and even then, only for lunch. Cold cuts and burgers were not considered a dinner meal in Mother's book of real meals. Betty Crocker would have been proud of Martha Webb's attempt to keep dinner fresh and hearty, with everyone sitting down together, using matching white dishes and placemats. I often hated our healthy menu of steak, salad, and a vegetable every night. It was so boring.

Rory's dad had seven mouths to feed each day and he was a

milkman. Their family lived on potato chips, hotdogs, baked beans, and Kool-Aid. They had them for lunch and they had them for dinner. I prayed they would invite me to eat over at their house. I felt so fortunate when they did, because I was able to eat hotdogs and beans with their family. Not only did they have beans, wieners, chips, and cherry red Kool-Aid, they also had colorful plastic plates, with three pre-molded sections and 1950s style aluminum glasses in bright purple, blue, and green. I loved how the ice in the Kool-Aid made the aluminum glasses feel so cold on your lips.

To make the whole meal even better, they let me do the dishes in the kitchen sink after dinner! We had a built-in dishwasher at my house; we didn't get to do dishes and wear a dishtowel around our waists like an apron. It was always fun to eat at Rory's house.

When the Presidential Physical Fitness Award contest was announced, I knew I had a good chance of winning it. We already had the food part down pat at home. We certainly ate healthy meals and I was active and fit. I could envision the trophy or medals displayed in my room along with my other swimming and softball awards.

The qualifying events began the next week with sit-ups, push-ups, running, and throwing the softball. While we were doing each task in class and marking down our scores, I observed I was stronger, faster, more athletic, and physically fit than any of the other girls. Even the girls who had been good at sports in elementary school seemed to have lost their edge in the physical fitness department.

Girls who used to be able to throw a ball in a neighborhood baseball game now looked like they were throwing with their left hand. *What had happened to them?* I remember thinking. They throw like girls. I, on the other hand, threw the softball not only further than the entire yard measurements chalked on the cement playground, but over the chain link fence and into the bike racks. Now that's how to throw a ball.

This fitness test and the trophy would surely bring me honor and status, were my thoughts without actually thinking through the process. I will be almost popular, known throughout the whole school, maybe even become a legend. Unfortunately, my brain was functioning under the impression that each gym teacher would compile the scores and would bestow the award upon the winner in gym class. This was not how it played out. President John Fitzgerald Kennedy's Physical Fitness Award would be presented six weeks later during an all-school assembly.

On the day of the awards event, our principal, Mr. Hilter, or Hitler, as we called him because he marched around the campus with a no-nonsense look on his face, tapped on the microphone to get everyone's attention in the auditorium. Slowly, a muffled hush fell over the crowd, and what would end up being the worst moment of my twelve-year-old life began to unfold.

The moment I realized Hitler was actually going to hand out the awards, in the auditorium, in front of the whole school, the blood drained not only from my head and face, but it drained from my mind, arms, legs, and torso as if someone had just pulled the plug on my lifeblood supply. With his words, "Beginning with the seventh grade girls," everything began to happen in slow motion. Words slurred, lights blurred, and I swear I saw myself floating silently above the Bancroft Beavers Junior High School Auditorium wearing angel wings, wearing a flowing white robe, and playing a harp.

"That's you!" someone shouted in the distance. "Get up! Go!" Next, as I stumbled down the center aisle of the auditorium towards the stage, I heard what sounded like the entire school shouting, "Go, He Man!" "She's the Incredible Hulk!" "Help...please don't beat me up!" They probably said a lot more, but I was practicing disassociation from my physical body, so these are the only comments I remember.

I received the crappy, six-inch high, fake gold cup award from Hitler, and somehow made it back to my seat without actually falling down. So much for elevating my status to almost popular. Yeah, everyone knew my name and everyone took advantage of the opportunity to make me the brunt of jokes about jocks, lesbos, weightlifters, and bodybuilders.

For days, all the dorks in the school had a holiday while I was the victim of the week. Kids in junior high are merciless when one of their own is crippled. Darwin's concept 'survival of the fittest' must have first been coined to describe twelve to fourteen-year-olds before it was used in relationship to finches. Instead of proudly taking the trophy home, I dumped it in the first trashcan I could find, making a mental note for the future. It's best to throw like a girl.

Chapter Sixteen

AT BANCROFT JUNIOR HIGH School, every Bancroft Beaver had to shower after P.E. period. If you were normal, like five-feet-two-inches, had some pubic hair and developing breasts, this was probably embarrassing. If you were abnormally tall, with scant pubic hair and no breasts, this was akin to seeing yourself completely naked on a billboard across from the junior high school.

The P.E. teachers gave us padlocks for our gym lockers at the beginning of the school year and told us we should take the time to memorize our combination numbers. They explicitly instructed us to make sure the locks were closed and completely locked before we went out for class. The school was adamant each gym locker be closed and locked tight because there had been multiple incidents of theft in the locker room. They warned us that gym teachers would periodically roam the locker room while a class was out at P.E., and as a punishment for leaving your lock open, teachers would seize everything in the locker. Then they would take the contents to the head P.E. teacher's office for the remorseful and guilty student to reclaim.

Every girl in seventh period P.E. did indeed lock her gym locker with her padlock, since there was no hurry to get to another class. No one who had first through sixth period P.E. usually locked her padlock. In the mind of a twelve-year-old girl, opening your gym lock requires both memorization and manual dexterity. By the time you arrived at the locker room, you were already in a super hurry. You had to undress, put on your blue gym suit with snaps as buttons and bloomer bottoms, and make it out to where the class met for calisthenics, usually running to make it before the tardy bell.

Now, after class, the reverse was worse. When teachers dismissed us from class, they told us not to run back to the locker room. You had fifteen minutes to get back, check out a shower towel, take a shower, pass inspection, re-dress, fix your hair and makeup (okay, not me) and you still had to get to your next class before the tardy bell rang. Marathon runners couldn't accomplish that, let alone junior high school girls.

The Inspector General of the locker room shower was whichever P.E. teacher had a free period. They'd sit on the five-foot high wall of the shower entrance and inspect your body to make sure you looked wet. If you didn't look wet, they'd blow a loud whistle and tell you to hit the showers again, this time 'with water!' Lots of girls got caught but being naked and sent back to the showers was far worse for anyone who was tall, skinny, and breast-less. To avoid trouble, I was never naked a moment longer than necessary and I always got completely wet.

I figured out that by taking a shower and actually getting wet, I'd save the time of being sent back, thus adding minutes to the narrow window of time to get to my next class. Though we had all been warned about leaving our locks unlocked, I thought by not locking my gym lock, but making it look like it was locked, I'd add another few precious seconds towards my escape to the next period—a familiar thought pattern of most incarcerated half-wits. In September, October, and November, this worked, making the lock look like it was locked, but with a sharp yank, it would quickly open. No problem. Time saved.

Right before Christmas vacation, my luck ran out. We were out on the field, playing field hockey. This particular activity was a real time taker because shin guards and the hockey stick had to be checked out at the beginning of the class and checked back in at the end of the period. We'd have to place the sticks in one garbage can, put our shin guards in another, and if you were assigned the position of goalie, you had a mask and chest gear that went into another can. Returning the equipment took valuable time, so all the girls totally ignored the 'do not run' warning, stampeding back to the locker room and showers, in hopes of making it to their next period before the tardy bell.

On one particular day, I ran with the bulls towards the locker room door, grabbed a towel, hit the showers, got completely wet, and passed inspection easily. I headed towards my locker and noticed it was wide open and there was nothing inside. For a moment, I thought maybe I was in the wrong row of lockers. Panicking, I checked again. No, right row...right locker...oh, crap...

Wrapped in this little tiny gym towel, I made my way awkwardly towards the head P.E. teacher's office. I didn't know if I was more concerned that I'd been caught or that one of the teachers had actually touched my bra and underwear. Standing in front of the teacher's office in basically a dishtowel and still dripping from the shower, I faced my accuser.

"Didn't you know the rule that all locks had to be locked?" Asked the teacher.

"Yes, ma'am," I answered, trying to sound apologetic.

"Did you know someone might steal something from your locker?"

"Yes." (Who would want a "Show and Grow" bra?)

"Did you know your parents will be notified of this infraction?"

"Yes." (My grandmother will say it's more evidence of my diminished mental state.)

"Have you learned your lesson?" She said, sounding like she wasn't sure I had.

"Yes, ma'am." (Probably not. The next period just comes too fast for me to adapt.)

"Are you sorry you tried to skirt the rules?" She was still questioning my sincerity.

"Yes." (No, not really—just sorry I got caught.)

"Are you going to do this again?" She asked, cocking her head.

"No, ma'am." (At least for a while.)

"Do you know your combination number?" She finally asked.

"It's something like 30-40-62…or 40-32-60…or…"

"Okay, take your things and get dressed. You better memorize your combination numbers as soon as possible."

Reaching my next class ten minutes late, I opened the classroom door quietly and stood in the doorframe at the back of the class where everyone with a last name starting with W-Z always sat. Waiting for my friend Joanne Walker to look up and see me hiding there; she finally looked up and quickly recognized I needed her to help me sneak into my seat when the teacher was facing the blackboard.

After a few moments, Joanne started to nod her head for me to slip into my seat unnoticed, but quickly changed it to a "No!" when the teacher suddenly turned and faced the class. By now, Jerky Jerry Winslow also noticed I was hiding just inside the door. Jerry was one of the biggest kiss-ass kids I'd ever known—the poster child of teacher's pets. Loved by the staff for his never-ending tattling, but hated by the kids, he'd taken many a punch for his annoying habits. Looking at me, he jetted his right hand up in the air, practically stood up, and began frantically waving while grunting, trying to get the teacher's attention. Sensing it was now or never, I slunk in, while La Profesora was writing on the blackboard.

Of course, now I was very late to Spanish class and Senora

Domingo, in her exaggerated, high-pitched, singsong voice, made a bad situation worse by confronting me in Spanish as I tried to sneak in the back door of the classroom unnoticed.

"Hola, Susanna!" she said. "Como esta? Porque llegas tarde? Te vere en las detencion de hoy. Verdad? Detention this afternoon," she said, making eye contact, just in case my Spanish was poor.

"Si, Senora Domingo," I said looking down at the floor as Jerky Jerry grinned like the Cheshire cat.

* * *

After school, I went to the detention hall to do my time, along with every other school screw up, juvenile delinquent, dumb kid, and class clown. The hands on the clock moved unnaturally slow while we waited for the forty-five-minute period to pass. Knowing I was in trouble for the lock fiasco when I got home, I didn't need a forty-five-minute delay in the penalty phase.

By the time I arrived home from detention, of course, Mrs. Priget had already called my mom with the news of my failure to follow the school's golden rule, 'Always lock your gym lock.' My mother's interpretation of my infraction went more along the lines of my potential for a lifetime of criminal activities. She was also embarrassed a school official called our home, one more time, over something I'd done.

"Don't you know, Susan, they have rules for reasons?" asked my mother.

"Yeah, I know."

"Daddy and I expect our kids to follow rules. It's embarrassing for the school to call and say one of our children is not a rule follower. That reflects on us negatively as parents and role models."

Oh, come on, this doesn't mean anything. I just tried to make sure I got to my next period class. Jeez...not that I'll end up in jail by the time I'm sixteen. "Okay, Mom, okay. I'll lock my lock and be late for Spanish. That will make it look like I'm a rule follower. Is that what you want?" I replied sarcastically.

"Don't get snippy with me, missy. I don't want to hear from the school about this again. Do you read me?"

"Yes. Over and out," I retorted, and retreated to my room. Things only got worse when unloading my notebook and textbooks I found my library book was missing and there was a book report due the next day.

The gym teacher must have taken it when she stripped my locker and it got left in her office. Since elementary school, I always chose one of three subjects for my reports: sharks, witches, or how a cow's stomach works. A wide variety of topics in my mind, but none appropriate for this English report. Crap. All I needed was for Mom to find out my library book was still in the P.E. teacher's office and she'd start a new tirade on my level of irresponsibility. No problem, I'd just have to find a book at home to skim read and write a report.

Fortunately, we had lots of books in our den covering a variety of topics. One was on African tribes that I'd already read a chapter or two and decided I could skim read a few more and begin my report. If one of the unfortunate students picked to give their report orally, I could at least show the pictures of Africa. Pictures, especially colored ones, always helped to make an oral report better. Things were looking up.

With my written report and the book on Africa, I went to school the next day feeling fairly solid. Chances were I might not get picked to read my report aloud because the teacher had told us we were only going to spend one period listening to students give their reports orally. In gym class, I locked my gym lock tightly as instructed, and even made it to Spanish class on time. The day was going better than usual, then off to English class. The teacher asked if everyone had his or her reports and the classroom all nodded in unison.

"Was there anyone who wanted to read his or her report aloud and get extra credit for volunteering?" questioned Mr. Mason. Jerky Jerry Winslow raised his hand and grunted excitedly.

"No!" moaned the classroom.

"Yes, Jerry! Good! Go right ahead, son," said the teacher.

Jerky Jerry gave a boring report on England and showed a book with crummy black and white line drawings of some ugly king and queen. No one asked to have his book passed around, so Jerry asked the teacher if he would like to see the book.

"Well, of course, Jerry, that was an interesting topic for sure, and very relevant because this is, as you all know, English class! We wouldn't be here if it wasn't for jolly ol' England!" More moans from the class.

"Ten extra points for Jerry for volunteering to be the first and for such a good report! Does anyone else want to volunteer?" he asked the silent crowd. "Okay, Bobby and Karen are the next two oral reports."

"Susan Webb, you're up next," droned Mr. Mason. By now, he was as bored as we were from listening to the seemingly endless string of boring topics. The good news, I thought, was no one was paying attention and they wouldn't notice any mistakes. My report was about tribes of Africa, and I was surprised to see the class was paying attention. I figured they were listening because I told them one tribe was rumored to be actual cannibals, and that caught their attention.

I showed the map of Africa, and one kid asked to see the book to look at pictures. I handed him the book, glad to be able to sit back down. As another student gave his report, I noticed Jerky Jerry was showing the pictures in my African book to some other kids and they were snickering. Mr. Mason, growing increasingly annoyed at the ruckus caused by the boys, stopped the class and asked Jerry to state the problem.

"They're naked!" said Jerky Jerry with unabashed glee.

"Yeah, you can see the ladies' boobies and the men's peckers!" announced someone else.

Mr. Mason was completely confused, and the class was now in a frenzy, excitedly muttering the words 'boobies and peckers.' Everyone was trying to get a look at my book. What the heck was happening? The teacher grabbed the book and the period bell mercifully rang with a loud buzz. Everyone who hadn't seen the photos shuffled out of the class, trying to locate someone who had. Jerry, who was such a dimwit was an instant celebrity.

Mr. Mason was holding my book and scanning the photos. "These photos are not appropriate for school, Susan," he scolded. "They show natives in various states of partial dress and some with no clothes at all. Did you read this whole book? I don't see how you couldn't have noticed these photographs were too graphic to be shown to your classmates. This will require a phone call to your parents immediately."

Two phone calls in a week, what are the chances? Big deal, who hasn't seen pictures of boobies and peckers? Plus the photos are dark and grainy and don't really show much. Jeez...

Next, Mr. Mason told our principal, Mr. Hilter, about the photos in the book. However, he actually hadn't seen the pictures, so Mr. Hilter thought the whole book was of photographs of nude men and women. Because of the gravity of the situation, the principal decided he would personally call home and inform my parents about my nasty and graphic book.

I could only imagine my mother's reaction to his phone call. A book of naked people? Susan brought a book of naked people to Bancroft Junior High School? How could this happen? When I arrived home, I knew there was going to be trouble, but not knowing Mr. Hilter had described the African tribe book as if it was a book comprised totally of naked people, I was thrown off when I opened the front door. My mom was sitting on the sofa, stoned faced and frozen. For a second, I thought she might have suffered a stroke after receiving the call from the school. My grandmother, in the kitchen making her afternoon cup of tea, had overheard the call, and had held onto key words like nude and photos.

"Where did you get such filth and why would you take such vial trash to school?" asked my mother, coming out of her coma, demanding to see the book. I handed her the African tribe book.

"What is this?" she asked the obvious question.

"The book I used for my oral report," I responded matter-of-factly.

"Mr. Hilter said you brought a book of naked people to school today, Susan, not a book on Africa."

"This is the book, Mom. The report was on African tribes. I took the book to show the colored map of Africa, to get extra credit. I didn't know about the photos of the natives. I never noticed the photos since I only skim-read the book because my real book was still at school in the gym teacher's office."

I tried to explain how this whole mess was directly connected to the gym locker incident, but somehow she didn't see the connection as clearly as I did. Her focus was on how embarrassed she was the school had called to notify her my book had multiple pictures of nasty nude photos. It was obvious she was already imagining a visit with me in prison, sitting stoically behind a glass window with only a phone for communication, our hands touching both sides of the glass while my mother softly cried.

My parents always used the anatomical words for various body parts, but my mom's descriptions of the photos, peppered with the words breast and penises, made me way more embarrassed than boobies and peckers, which I could have endured. After a few minutes, she was mad I took a book on Africa, but relieved it wasn't actually a book with filthy, trashy, graphic, color photos. Of course, my grandmother was listening to the conversation.

"Let me see that book, Martha," she demanded, assured there was more to the story than I was revealing. She focused on the grainy pictures and exclaimed, "Good Lord, Martha, why would you allow such a book in your home? You already know she's not right upstairs." She pointed at her head and tapped it with her bent finger. "You know she don't have a lick of sense about what's appropriate or not. Why even have such books? My God, Martha...what were you thinking?"

I don't know what my mom was thinking, but I felt sorry for her. As my grandmother went on and on about her theories of what was wrong with me, thoughts of, "Just shut the heck up, Granny!" filled my head. My guess is my mom was thinking along the same lines.

Chapter Seventeen

A FEW MONTHS INTO the new school year, my friend Vicky announced her parents were going to let her have a sleepover party for her thirteenth birthday. About twelve of us got invitations, and it sounded like it would be really fun to spend the night at someone's house, since Katy and I no longer had sleepovers because we went to different schools.

By the beginning of November, many of us seventh graders were functioning like zombies. What we thought was going to be a great new school year in junior high had morphed into a living hell. Homework was so much harder than elementary school, and changing classes, combination locks, what to wear, and how to wear it were just overwhelming. Personally, I needed a break. Vicky's invitation to her slumber party was just that ticket. Excited at the prospect of a whole twelve hours away from home as close as next weekend made me giddy with possibilities. I delivered the invitation to my mom, and she started the inquisition.

"Is she a nice girl?" (She's not a recent felon, to my knowledge.)

"Are her parents going to be there the entire time?" (Yeah, when they're not at the bar.)

"Do you know the other girls who are going?" (How do I know? It's Vicky's party.)

"Are you planning on leaving the premises?" (Yes, immediately, but I'll be home eventually.)

"For crying out loud. Just call her mom then you can ask her all these questions. You make everything out to be such a big deal. Jeez, you should have been a cop!"

"I just want to make sure it's supervised, Susan."

"I just want to make sure you have a terrible time, Susan," I mumbled under my breath.

The next week dragged by until Saturday night finally rolled around. By six in the evening when the sleepover started, I was so happy to be away from my parents. Vicky's mother told us to all take our sleeping bags and overnight bags out to their garage, which they had remodeled into a family room. Someone turned the radio to the Top Forty and we all began to sing, dance, and gyrate around the room. There was so much going on and the music was so loud, I hadn't noticed some of the girls who arrived late. One particular girl was really pretty. I wondered who she was. Jumping back up to dance some more, I found myself trying to look at her without being obvious, which of course made it more obvious. By now, girls were collapsing and falling to the floor, tired from all the movement.

"Let's play some games," someone suggested.

"No, let's have a contest where everyone does their partner's makeup and hair," proposed someone else.

Let's not, I said to myself. Unfortunately, the makeup contest won out and all the girls sat down.

"Everyone pair up," said Vicky, as I moved to the outside of the circle. No, I thought, not a makeup contest, as I tried not to look uncomfortable. Then there was a tap on my shoulder.

"Wanna be my partner?" The pretty girl said to me.

"Ah, yeah, sure," I replied, not knowing what else to say. "Just so you know, I'm not very good at this makeup stuff."

"Me neither," she said, smiling. "We'll teach each other, okay?"

"Uh-huh." I tried to control my nervousness. "So how does this work?"

"You sit cross-legged and I'll put my legs over yours, then you'll be close enough for me to reach your face. How does that sound? Or do you want to do me first?"

"No, you go first, but don't make me look stupid, okay?"

"I'd never try to make you look stupid," she said, laughing. "And by the way, my name is Liz; I'm Vicky's friend from elementary school."

"I'm Susan. I know Vicky from our school."

A huge container of all kinds of makeup and hair products appeared in the center of the circle of girls who had paired off and they were perched just like us with one girl's legs over the crossed legs of the other. It appeared that a few of the participants knew what they were doing, but for the most part I was relieved that most didn't look very confident with their abilities either.

"Close your eyes. I'm going to put eyeshadow on your eyelids. Should I use Sultry Slate or Exotic Blue?" Liz asked as if I had a preference.

"Sultry Slate sounds like ground up rock so I think I'd prefer Exotic

Blue, madam.," I answered, smiling.

"Well, I also have Jungle Green as an option," she said, giggling, "and you do have pretty green eyes." No one had ever said my eyes were pretty. To me they looked like little pig eyes, small and slanted. Not pretty in any way. It felt so weird when she said my eyes were pretty. I never thought of anything about myself as being attractive.

"Okay, now mascara. Hold still, you're moving," said Liz.

"Ow, you poked me in the eye with that thing. It burns! Be careful!" I rubbed my eye with my fist.

"Then stop moving around or you'll get poked again," replied Liz, now cracking up and placing her hand on the back of my neck to steady my head. "I said hold still!"

"I am. Hurry up."

"God, you're a pain, Susan. Now for lipstick."

"Oh no, not lipstick; do something else."

"If we're gonna win, you need lipstick and your hair done, okay?" said Liz seriously.

"We don't need to win anyways, and this is enough of a makeover for my taste. You can stop anytime—like now!"

"Shut up, sit still, close your eyes, and let me do your lipstick. Now you can open them."

When I opened my eyes, Liz's face was less than a foot away from mine. All I could focus on were her lips. They were the prettiest lips I'd ever seen. Hardly breathing and so struck by her beauty, I continuing to stare.

"What are you staring at?" asked Liz. "I'm supposed to be looking at you. Now let me do your hair."

I was unable to argue, though I felt like I should to stay in character, but I just sat mutely while she put my hair up into a French roll, sticking bobby pins in to secure the do. Finally, she stuck in a pin that stabbed my scalp, and awoke me from my stupor.

"Ow, you just stabbed me in the head!"

"Sorry, didn't mean to. I'm almost done. I think it looks great. Let me put some hairspray on it," she stated, engulfing me in a haze of smelly, sticky spray while handing me a mirror. "You look just like Audrey Hepburn!" Liz exclaimed, breaking into a loud rendition of Moon River, causing everyone else in the room to stop and look at us.

Audrey Hepburn? I was more comfortable along the lines of George Peppard. In no way did I want to look like Audrey Hepburn. I was shocked as I glanced in the mirror. I don't know if I looked like

Audrey Hepburn, but I sure didn't look like myself. *Who is that?*

"Okay, that's enough. Take it down, Liz," I said, trying not to sound harsh.

"No, we're gonna win the contest."

"No, we're not," I said quietly. "I don't want to look like Audrey Hepburn. I want to look like me." I began to wipe off the eye shadow and lipstick with a tissue.

Liz's previously beautiful lips were beginning to pout and she looked like she was about to cry as she ran to the backyard. I followed her outside.

"I'm sorry, Liz, you did a great job. I'm just not comfortable looking like this, okay? It's nothing about you; it's about me. Please don't get your feelings hurt. It's no big deal." Though she said it was okay, I knew it wasn't. I'd hurt her feelings with my reaction, and it felt bad.

"Hey," I said brightly, "I'll make you up, if you'd like. I'm positive we'll win the contest 'cause you're already so pretty. You tell me how to do it, I'll follow your instructions, and I just know we'll win! I bet I'm a Max Factor makeup wiz in disguise." By now, she was starting to smile and I felt like it was going to be all right.

"I get it; you're not a girlie-girl, Susan. I should've known you wouldn't be interested in looking like Audrey Hepburn. I'm sorry."

"There's nothing to be sorry about. I'm not into being a lady movie star like her, but I did like the movie," I said, breaking into my own rendition of Moon River, singing directly to Liz, my new crush. "Let's go back inside," pulling her gently by the arm back towards the family room door, I noticed she didn't pull away from me. Later that night, she slipped a folded piece of paper with her phone number into my hand. Maybe my life wasn't so lousy.

Chapter Eighteen

AS I MENTIONED BEFORE, my mom associated makeup and ratted hair with women of the night or the streets. Who knows why, since to my best recollection she didn't personally know any women who were prostituting themselves. Nonetheless, she seemed quite knowledgeable on the topic.

Girls with poor morals also wore red silk underpants, she insisted. To me there wasn't any connection between red underwear and morals, but apparently, my mom knew of a connection of which I wasn't aware. Since my parents didn't socialize with any other couples, I could only figure my maternal grandmother had been the source of this information on women in the service industry—what they wore, how they ratted their hair, and how they fixed runs in nylons with fingernail polish.

I complained incessantly about wanting to tease my hair like every other girl in junior high. Finally, one day my mom came to me with a compromise. She would help me put 'material' in my hair to make it look like it was ratted, but this would spare my own hair from getting split ends.

"What's the 'material' we are talking about?" I questioned hesitantly, slightly squinting. My mother explained that a few months back she had rediscovered my ponytail that was cut off in second grade, which she'd been saving in her lingerie drawer. Knowing how much I wanted to rat my hair like the other girls, she had taken some of my ponytail hair, combed, and ratted it into two wads. This way, she continued on, we wouldn't have to actually rat one single hair on my head, but these could be placed under my hair to give it height.

She then produced two wads that could only be described as very large cat hairballs, minus saliva. She proceeded to stick one wad on the side of my hair with a hairpin, and then pulled my hair over it, giving the illusion my hair was ratted underneath. My first intuition was major skepticism, but I was also desperate to blend in like every other girl at school with teased and sprayed hair.

Against my better judgment and forgetting my previous promise to never let her 'help' me again, the following morning she inserted the hairballs on both sides of my head with hairpins. I pulled my hair over the top of them and then thoroughly sprayed them with hairspray to freeze their positions.

Starting out, it really didn't look terrible. Not exactly like everyone else's, but close enough to make me think I could pass. At thirteen, I was still so trusting, even after all the things my mom had inadvertently done to humiliate me, I left for school thinking I actually looked pretty normal, just as she had assured me.

For the first few hours of the day, no one said anything, which I optimistically took as a good sign. At least, it must not be super obvious there were two hairballs under my own hair. I made it all the way to gym class without detection, and was feeling quite self-assured, but that confidence was about to end.

After suiting up for gym and heading out to the field, the teacher asked me to lead the warm-up calisthenics. Not thinking, I picked jumping jacks, and after only five or six jumps, the hairballs began to bounce around under my own hair. The more jumping jacks we did, the more the hairballs loosened from their confinements and began trying to escape. By the time number twenty arrived, one mass had begun to move about freely. By the count of thirty, the other wad was free and dangling precariously over my ear. At this point, the cat was out of the bag, so to speak, and I knew there was no reasonable way to explain why these huge hairballs were clinging to my head.

Of course, my fellow gym students noticed them immediately, and began to squeal and say, "Look at her hair...it's coming out in clumps!"

"She's going bald!" others from the calisthenics line said, joining in. Piranhas! It was hard to maintain order as the lead warm up instructor when people are shouting and pointing at your hairballs. Mercifully, they dropped out in two wads. Unceremoniously, I shoved them into the pocket of my gym shorts and silently swore never to trust my mother again. No more fake ratting in my hair. From now on, it would be real ratted hair and no imitations, I swore to myself, mentally crossing my heart.

Finding out shortly into seventh grade that doing well in P.E. activities meant immediate social alienation and to survive socially, you needed to at least appear interested in boys, and to join in school activities. I was beginning to get the picture. It didn't matter if you were smart, athletic, or a good person. What mattered was blending in.

We had a school pep squad, which was composed of four girl cheerleaders and a boy cheerleader named Casey Anderson. In addition to the pep squad, seven more girls held up cardboard letters spelling out the word 'BEAVERS' in all caps at all of the boy's intramural sports games. Thinking this would be a way for me to participate in a school activity, I decided to try out for the squad after school, hoping to win a spot holding one of the letters.

It was immediately evident that if I held any of the letters at my chest level, it would be almost a foot higher than any of the other letters unless all the other girls held theirs above their heads. This might have worked, but then my head protruded from the top of my sign. Wouldn't work, the judges told me as gently as they could. Wouldn't look professional, they murmured in unison. Yeah, well, we wouldn't want to look unprofessional, 'cause we're the Bancroft Damn Beavers. Okay, yeah, I understood.

I moped all the way home about my failure to secure a place on the letter squad. Nothing ever seemed to go my way, I thought glumly. I changed out of my school clothes, then began my homework. Opening my desk to get a pencil, I noticed a folded piece of paper, then realized it was the phone number Liz had slipped into my hand the night of Vicky's party. After running through all my doubts about calling her, I decided what the heck. It had been such a lousy day, what was the worst that could happen besides she'd forgotten me?

Retrieving the phone, I threaded the cord under my bedroom door and then closed it tightly. Nervously, I dialed the number on the paper, and the phone rang and rang for what seemed like fifteen minutes when someone on the other end finally picked it up.

"Ah, is, ah, Liz there?" I asked.

"No, Liz won't be home for another half hour, can I take your name?"

"Will you tell her Susan called? I'll call back in an hour, if that's okay."

"Okay, will do. I'll tell her Susan called and she'll call back." Click went the phone.

As the minutes ticked on, I started to get really nervous about how the conversation might actually go. Wonder if she didn't remember me, what if she decided she didn't like me. Wonder if she had a boyfriend now. Wonder. Wonder. Wonder. I'm not calling back, I decided; it's already been a terrible day. Then the phone rang. Picking up the receiver slowly, I mumbled, "Hello?" There was a split second of silence then someone softly humming Moon River.

"Hey you!"

"Hey you, yourself! What's up? I'm so glad you called. I've been thinking about you," said Liz.

"Yeah, me too. Today was so sucky, I needed to talk to someone friendly. I hate my life. Let me tell you what happened. It started this morning in P.E. class..."

An hour later, my mother interrupted my cozy little world by knocking rudely on my door, telling me to get off the phone because she had to make a call. So much for my fleeting blissful retreat from the real world. It was back to reality.

"I gotta go. My mom needs to use the phone."

"Call me later in the week?" asked Liz.

"Definitely." I felt like I just received a lifesaving blood transfusion. I had somebody who understood to trade stories about how crappy life could get and we laughed about it. I loved her for understanding me.

Chapter Nineteen

PART OF SEVENTH GRADE P.E. class was a Sex Education component. When this unit was about to begin, the teachers sent home a packet of information listing what would be covered and asking parents to give permission to let their child attend. There was a small paragraph with a box to check, inviting parents to join their child for the final class, but no one paid attention to it because no parent had ever come to Sex Education in the history of Bancroft Junior High School.

The anticipation of this class, known around school as 'Sexed Ed.,' washed excitedly over the entire seventh grade class as the permission slips went home. During this time, the girls got flirtier as they teased the boys, and the boys became more foul-mouthed. Every known sexual buzzword was continually uttered in the halls between classes, at breaks, and during lunch. Words, which many of us had never heard, let alone used, floated between groups of boys and girls at a rate that was electrifying, expanding our vocabulary daily to new heights. If the goal of the class was to make us more responsible, I would say that particular goal wasn't met.

Teachers and administrators warned us if the inappropriate language and taunting did not stop, some students were going to be banned from the class. Because no one wanted to miss out, we all stopped shouting nasty words at each other, and resorted to just writing and passing dirty notes.

During the weeks prior to Sexed Ed. classes, Roman O'Malley and Cash Jovivian became very popular boys. Cash was this little scrappy kid who spent weekends living out scenes from West Side Story with his large clan of Puerto Rican relatives. He was little in stature but dressed like a hoodlum in jeans and a black leather jacket, and smoked cigarettes off campus. It was even rumored he carried a switchblade in his pocket and a rubber in his wallet. If you believed Cash, he and his cousins were members of the Puerto Rican Kings gang, and each weekend would get drunk and fight with rival gangs using clubs, knives, and bicycle chains.

Every school morning, he'd cruise into homeroom wearing sunglasses. The morning fog could be so thick you couldn't see your hand in front of your face, but Cash would arrive wearing his cool sunglasses. At lunch period on Mondays, the boys would surround him to hear him describe what the PRKs had done over the weekend. None of the kids knew of any other seventh grader who said he was in a gang, wore a leather jacket, and carried a switchblade knife, so Cash was a popular storyteller at Bancroft Junior High.

Occasionally, he'd come to school with a black eye or a cut on his face that he'd point to as evidence of the weekend's fight with another gang. If you also believed Cash, he claimed to have already had sex with a variety of girls. Big, fat ones with giant 'che ches' were his favorite, he boasted. I personally could not imagine little tiny Cash having sex with any big fat girl with giant boobs without the risk of being accidentally crushed or smothered. I could buy the Puerto Rican gang stuff because of how he looked and talked, but the sex part I had difficulty believing. Though some of the other kids thought he was exaggerating the sex stuff too, no one was about to argue the point and risk getting shanked right there at the lunch tables.

Once Ricky De Valle, who was in ninth grade and was supposedly associated with a Mexican gang, challenged Cash to prove he was having sex. He told Cash to bring some kind of evidence to school the following Monday to prove he had gotten laid over the weekend. Cash, not one to back down over anything, agreed to the challenge. For the remainder of the week, there was great speculation as to what Cash could possibly bring to school that would provide evidence that he had sex over the weekend. By Friday, between the upcoming Sexed Ed. class and Ricky's challenge to Cash, most of the school was jittery with excitement.

Monday morning, Cash arrived wearing his signature sunglasses, swaggering ever so slightly as he entered homeroom. The boys were eager to hear his stories and dying to see the evidence of his deed, but he produced no evidence. The bell rang, and school began. At lunch, Ricky approached Cash and a large group of kids began to form around them, pushing to get as close as possible to see what evidence would be produced.

According to a kid who had a front row view, Ricky raised his hand and a hush fell over the crowd. Then to everyone's total shock, Cash pulled a gigantic pair of bright red, silk underwear from the pocket of his leather jacket, and dangled it in front of Ricky's stunned face. The group let out a collective gasp, and then went totally silent again, as Cash let the underpants fall to the ground and then sauntered away. One boy claimed the crowd was so stunned, no one moved or said a word for almost a minute, and then he said the panties just disappeared without a trace.

What happened after that varied upon who told the story. Somebody said the red undergarment ended up in the trash, Jerky Jerry insisted it ended up on the principal's desk, and another kid said he saw a boy throw them on the roof of the school. Mattie Carpenter said she saw the red panties in the Lost and Found box in the front office, though that seemed highly unlikely to me. Who would have had the nerve to walk into the office and turn in a gigantic pair of red, girl's silk underwear?

After school that day, Cash walked off campus, lit up a cigarette and headed to the liquor store, where one of his older brothers always picked him up in a low rider car. To me, it looked like he had grown an inch or two taller that day. Regardless of what you believed, Cash *was* cool.

The only topic the remainder of that day and most of the following week was the rumors about the giant red underpants. Student's theories ranged from what girl they belonged, to wild stories about where they actually came from.

By Thursday morning, the school staff was so sick of the tales that an emergency staff meeting was called at lunch to discuss how to squelch all the school rumors so students could get back to the task of learning. They decided all homeroom teachers should address the issue first period, and 'put the rumors to bed,' so to speak. I'm not sure they got the irony of this statement, though our snorting and laughing should have been a clue. All I could think was, oh my God, my mom had been right all along. Loose girls do wear red underpants.

Another popular boy during the seventh grade Sex Education unit was Roman O'Malley, who came to our school when his entire family immigrated from Ireland. Roman was labeled a slow learner by the school administration and just plain dumb by the rest of the student body. Roman was two years older than most seventh graders, spoke with a heavy Irish accent, and he'd repeated seventh grade twice before. He was known for his excessive facial hair, which formed a prominent adult mustache. Even our school custodian didn't have as much facial hair as Roman.

To all the boys, being held back in seventh grade for two years translated to being the luckiest guy ever, as he'd gotten to take Sex Ed. multiple times. At lunchtime, seventh grade boys would surround him, and ask him questions about what he had already seen and learned in the previous classes.

"I really don't member much," he'd say, rocking back and forth and then from side to side, picking a pimple on his chin. "First, they talked about rubbers. Yeah, I think they did that," he said in his thick Irish brogue.

"Rubbers? They tell ya about rubbers? Like what about rubbers, Roman?" asked the boys excitedly.

"You know...about how to use 'em," he stammered on, picking his teeth with his fingernail. "You can blow them up like balloons, my cousin told me. That's how ya check for leaks," Roman said with authority.

"Leaks? What leaks? What else? Come on, Roman, try and remember more," the crowd pleaded.

"Next, they tell you how to jerk-off," he said, as if reading from a class outline. Then amending that statement, Roman admitted, "or that might've been my cousin Vinny who told me 'bout that."

"Who tells you how to jerk-off, your P.E. coach?" asked another kid. "Ah, that's so gross! Oh, my God!"

"Then I think they showed us some movies or something," said Roman, grinning. "I think they showed us a movie of peoples doin' it! Yeah, a boy was puttin' his thingy in a girl's thingy."

"What? No way," grumbled the crowd restlessly.

"You're lying, Roman," said Jerky Jerry accusingly.

"They don't show you nothin' like that! Ya probably saw your fat, ugly sister doing it!"

"No, they did!" Roman insisted, "or it looked like they were doin' it. You better take that back about my sister, Jerry, or I'll beat your ass! My sister's still a virgin! She went to Father Flannagan and confessed. Ma told us so. So she's still pure and savin' herself for a marriage."

Frankly, everyone knew Monica O'Malley was anything but a virgin. She had been seen humping boys in the alley behind Pan American Park and in cars by the high school. Vicky said she once saw her giving a guy a blowjob in the parking lot of Pappa Givanni's Pizza restaurant. Personally, I always wondered about these stories because Monica, like Roman, had sideburns and a partial beard herself.

Man, I thought, those guys must be really desperate. Years later, the rumor was she became a nun, though I found that difficult to imagine on more than one level. That convent must have really been hard up for new recruits, was all I could think. However, I did wonder if she owned a pair of red underpants before she enlisted in the order.

Roman's desire to say anything to please his fans eventually sidetracked his sudden rise in status as someone who had already experienced Sex Ed. After I heard what he told the boys, I realized Roman had probably never even attended the class. There was no way our school was going to teach us about the things he told the boys on the playground.

The first day of Sex Education class finally arrived. After assembling in the gym in our street clothes, gym teachers marched us off to a dark room with a projector and a pull-down audiovisual screen. Everyone wanted to sit up close to the screen, so there was a considerable amount of pushing and shoving as girls slid into the first few rows of seats. Our teachers shushed our excited titters and began the course by outlining what they were actually going to teach us and what they expected from the class. In solemn tones, they explained human sexuality was a normal part of growing up and it was important for us to know what was going to happen to both our bodies and to the bodies of the opposite sex. With that, the most anticipated class in junior high school began.

Delirious with excitement, the first day's lesson on pubic hair growth and body odor was something of a letdown. Not a girl in the class was the least bit interested in body hair or odor. We wanted the three P's—periods, penises, and premarital sex.

Day two was a discussion and eight-millimeter movie about starting your period. Now we're talkin'! They had the big diagrams of a girl's ram-like reproductive organs with everything labeled, using those words that only physician, medical students, or of course, my own mother actually ever uttered—vagina, uterus, fallopian tubes, and hormones. This was exciting, but we were hoping for a diagram of a boy's body too, but they didn't show us one. Pregnancy was still only alluded to, and rumor had it, actual sex and pregnancy were only discussed on the very last day of the class.

Day three was more about sanitary napkins versus tampons and feminine hygiene and bathing. Before the end of class, there was one quick reference to homosexual tendencies being deviant, which I chose to block out.

Somewhat disappointed by the first three days of the class, we were all hoping that on the fourth day, some more interesting material would come up. We had all heard rumors that on day five, there was a very explicit film shown that was embarrassing but informative. In addition, at the end of the film, we heard you could write anonymous notes with specific questions that the P.E. teachers would place on the overhead projector, so no one would know who had written them.

On Thursday, many of the girls were discussing what they wanted to ask and how to say it without giving their identity away. Explicit notes were found crumpled around the campus and we were beside ourselves with unbridled excitement and eager anticipation.

Finally, we were going to see the Famous Fifth Day Film. We'd finally be brought into the fold of the knowledgeable. Penises, pre-marital sex, and pregnancy, and we'd all be thoroughly sex educated. This all sounded so interesting and exciting that we could hardly contain ourselves. No other education took place in any other class that week at school because constant thoughts of sex and sexually related matters completely mesmerized everyone.

The infamous final day of the week arrived, and we filed into the dimly lit classroom confident there was going to be a film because the movie projector stood poised for action. Certainly, it was going to click off frames of information that none of us had ever imagined existed and would undoubtedly surpass body hair and odor by leaps and bounds. The excited chatter quieted; a crowd couldn't have more anticipated an academy award winning film. Then it began.

Flickering frames discussed a boy's anatomy in full detail. The word penis was written in large black letters along with new words like testicles, scrotum, wet dreams, the rhythm method for birth control, and finally, condoms. You could have heard a feather drop in the room. They kept the lights down low and began to pass around paper and pencils for us to use to write down our anonymous questions.

To make sure no one was singled out, we all had to fold up our papers, and the teacher instructed us to pass them up to the front where she would read appropriate questions, place them on the overhead projector, and we'd then have an open discussion.

The teacher unfolded the first question, but she apparently couldn't decipher what it said, because she stared at it and then put it aside. She placed the paper with the next question on the glass and projected it on the screen. It read, 'Tell us more about spurm.' Another girl had written a question about 'tampacks and losing your virginity.' Someone had written a question about 'boy's night time evacuations and where they went.' The clarification of this question brought great rolls of giggling. Another student requested clarification if the 'rhythm method of birth control had anything to do with music.' One more placed on the overhead projector asked, 'Is a rubber like a rubber band that you put around the end of the penis so nothing can squirt out?' By now, almost everyone in the class was snickering and chuckling at the questions.

Then the teacher placed the very last and final question on the glass of the projector and focused. It read in perfect handwriting, 'Do girls begin their menstruation at about the same age their mother started theirs?' At least half of the girls in class still had no clear understanding of what menstruation actually was, and certainly didn't want to imagine that their mothers had it too. That was way too much information in my mind. Who the heck would have written that question?

I turned around to see who was sitting behind me in the classroom. As I squinted my eyes to focus in the darkened room, my stomach dropped to my feet. I saw a familiar shaped woman sitting in the very back row. Gasping aloud, I thought I was going to have a stroke and die on the spot. Blood rushed to my head and I had trouble maintaining my balance in the chair. As soon as the blood filled my head, the blood then backwashed out at an even faster speed, leaving me with a death grip on my chair, trying not to faint.

Other girls were looking at me and I saw their lips moving, but heard nothing except a loud roaring in my ears. My friends looked frightened and confused as I wobbled back and forth between a stroke or fainting. The period bell rang, but I could only remain at my desk with my head flopped forward. I overheard girls asking, "Whose mother was that?" followed by "I'd die if my mom came to Sex Ed. class! How rank!"

Remember, I said no mother had ever attended the Sex Ed. class in the history of Bancroft Junior High School. Well, that was until my mother decided to show up. Only Martha Webb would have misinterpreted the box about parents attending on the permission slip to mean parents were actually invited to attend and show up. Could my life get any worse? I couldn't believe she came.

The questions about whose mother came to class lingered into the next week. Fortunately, no one in my P.E. class knew my mother yet, so no one else knew it was my mom. To perpetuate the secret, I repeatedly asked the same question, "Whose mother came?" to everyone, figuring this would end anyone thinking it was my own mother who once again betrayed me.

When the class finally ended, the other topic that seemed to take on a life of its own was the topic of homosexuality. After the class, there were more references to fags and queers thrown around by the boys. I really had no idea what they were talking about except that some of the boys said that the English teacher, Mr. Cohen, 'was light in his loafers,' which my friend explained was meant to imply he was a homosexual. The only thing I'd ever noticed about Mr. Cohen was he looked like he'd never spent a day in his life in sunshine. To me, he was just this pale, quiet, English teacher who constantly told me to stop talking in his class.

Boys, particularly loud-mouthed Sam Shatole, or Shithole, as we outcastes knew him, made fun of guys who were quiet, studious, and lousy at athletics by calling them gay, or fairies to make them feel embarrassed. To my knowledge, none of those guys were actually gay. Some of the older girls said Miss Evanstan, one of the ninth grade P.E. teachers, and Miss Walker, an eighth grade coach, were lezzies. To me they were just cool teachers that chose to wear Bermuda shorts rather than skirts while teaching classes. When the girls referred to them as lezzies, I thought they said lizzies, figuring it had something to do with a P.E. teacher who liked other women and maybe lizards or reptiles. Though still confused, when it came up in conversations, I too began to nod knowingly; yup, they're lizzies.

One time, for some bizarre reason during a family dinner, the topic of homosexuality came up. Feeling very cool, I confidently announced Miss Evanstan and Miss Walker, two of the girls' P.E. teachers, were lizzies. My mother stopped eating and my father just stared blankly at me. Having no idea what I was talking about, I didn't know I had just made a statement that absolutely no one else at the dinner table understood.

"What's a 'lizzie,' Susan?" my mother asked.

"You know, Mom," I replied knowingly, nodding my head like an expert on the topic, "she is a lizzie," putting emphasis on each word.

"What are you talking about?" Randy asked. "What's a 'lizzie'?"

"If you weren't so stupid, you'd know," I said, screwing up my face as if this fact was so well known that even the developmentally delayed, such as my brother, should have been aware of it.

Still paused with her fork in midair, my mom asked me again, "What did you just say?" Puzzled as to why she was so serious, I began to worry I might have made a mistake.

"She's a lizzie." This time I spoke with less confidence.

"I hear the word, Susan, but what does the word really mean?"

"It's...ah...it's a woman who teaches P.E., collects and breeds lizards and other reptiles, and also... ah... likes only to be friends with other lady P.E. teachers who collect lizards." I made my statement with my voice dropping off because I wasn't actually sure it meant she only liked lizards or other reptiles and I didn't want to be embarrassed if I was wrong. Dad resumed eating his dinner and my brother resumed shaking his head, mumbling under his breath that I was an idiot, while my mom just blinked.

"We'll talk later," she said almost in a whisper. I was certain this was not going to be a good conversation for either one of us.

Later she came to my room to talk. "Who told you about lesbians?" She asked.

"I don't 'member."

"Do you want me to explain more to you?"

"No," I said shaking my head vigorously. The thought of my parents having sex, which I knew for a fact they didn't, could only rival the thought of my mother discussing lesbians.

"It has nothing to do with lizards, Susan".

"Okay," I said, guessing that at least I was right about it including other reptiles.

"Well, if you ever want more information on any sexual topic, I wish you would come directly to me," said my mom as she turned to leave my room.

"All right," I answered, staring at the floor. Oh yeah, that will happen about the same time hell freezes solid and opens a ski resort. Oh my God, I thought, as she closed my bedroom door. Talk to my mother about sex? Oh my God, how gross. Later in the evening, a repeating thought kept coming into my mind—I wonder if I'm a lezzie too?

Chapter Twenty

"HEY," YELLED VICKY ACROSS the schoolyard. "I have something for you. Liz asked me to give you an invitation to her birthday sleepover over Easter Vacation. Think you can go?"

"Yeah." I knew about it already from Liz, and after my mom interrogated me for hours while I sat at an old table, under a bare lightbulb, answering questions, she said I could go.

"Your mom is really strict," said Vicky. "I'm glad she's your mom and not mine."

"Yeah, I wish she was your mom and not mine too, but no such luck," I said as I headed for my next class. Excited about seeing Liz in person again, and thinking about how pretty she was, I completely tuned out the entire forty-five-minute history class, until the teacher said my name for the second time.

"Susan, are you listening or daydreaming?" my teacher asked, tapping the stick he used to point to the blackboard on my desk. *Daydreaming,* I thought, and then tried to look like I was listening.

Easter vacation was just a rehearsal for summer vacation in my mind. The weather was getting warmer, daylight savings beginning, and if none of our teachers ruined it by assigning some annoying spring project that had to be completed over every kid in the universe's objection, the vacation would be great. Unfortunately, that required all of our teacher's compliance to the plan, making the odds of a random assignment that would wreck our vacation plans increasingly possible as the final Friday approached. Particularly if you had science with Mr. Coleman sixth period. I loved science; even being his assistant sometimes in class, but that didn't mean I wanted to do a project over vacation. I mean, fruit flies were okay, but not particularly interesting in comparison to the week of free time Easter vacation promised.

So at the end of the period, when he silenced the class and pointed to the movie screen to expose the devastating news of the project to be done over the vacation, thirty pimply teenage foreheads simultaneously hit their desks in resignation. Up went the screen and on the board was written:

Why should you never tickle an egg? It might crack up!

What's the best way to catch the Easter Bunny? Hide and make a noise like a carrot!

What do you call a rabbit with fleas? Bugs Bunny!

Happy Easter vacation, everyone!

Mr. Coleman.

＊

Liz's slumber party was the last Friday of Easter week, and the invitation asked everyone to bring a dozen hard-boiled eggs to dye, along with your sleeping bag and overnight bag. At five p.m. on April fifteenth, everyone invited began to descend upon Liz's house for her birthday and sleepover party.

At Liz's mom's suggestion, we all dumped our sleeping bags in Liz's bedroom, along with piles of pajamas and jackets, and then went to their kitchen to begin dyeing dozens of Easter eggs. I made sure I stood right next to Liz at the dyeing table, and we happily bumped into each other while trying to get more dye on the eggs than on our fingers. Having dyed eggs many times before, this time it just seemed like so much more fun.

After we finished the eggs, everyone raced to the backyard to cook hotdogs and marshmallows and stuff ourselves with chips and sodas. I finished cooking one final gooey marshmallow, and returned to where I was sitting in the circle. As I was licking the last of my sticky fingers, an older and athletic looking girl sat down in the empty chair beside me.

"Hey, my name's Lauren. How do you know Liz? From school?"

"No," I said, stopping to wipe my mouth making sure there was no sweet remaining. "We met at a friend's birthday party at the beginning of the year. We've just become better friends over time and she invited me to her party."

"She's really cool, huh?" the girl said, smiling, "and not bad looking either."

"Yeah, she's great, and pretty too." I answered, just as Liz popped over to where we were sitting.

"This is who I was telling you about, Lauren. This is Susan."

"I thought so," Lauren replied, poking Liz in the ribs as she left the circle of chairs.

"What were you telling her about me?" I asked Liz as soon as

Lauren was out of hearing range. "Did you tell her that you made me look like I should have been on a Mardi Gras float at the other party?" now laughing.

"No, goofy, I told her that you were really nice and funny, and I liked being around you."

"Well, thanks for leaving out the makeup part, which I've been trying to block out of my memory for months. I'll probably need counseling for the rest of my life because of you," I said, now laughing even harder and falling to the ground.

"God, you are such an exaggerator. You didn't look that bad."

"I looked ridiculously unlike my true self," I said, trying to feign indignation, but now laughing so hard I was gasping for a breath. "Definitely not the real me."

"Get up, you dork," said Liz, lightly kicking me in my side as I rolled around on the ground. "I've had enough of the 'real you' for now. I'm going inside. Some girls want to play Truth or Dare, and they've already put questions into a hat."

Everyone was already drawing numbers when I finally got up off the ground and came back into Liz's bedroom. I was handed the hat and withdrew the final piece of folded up paper. It read number eight. "Lucky number eight," I sang while dancing around the room.

Mavis picked the number one and chose truth over a dare.

Okay, the first question was, "Do you ever smell your armpits to see if you have B.O?" The room erupted into gag sounds. Who thought up that question? God. Gross.

"Never," exclaimed Mavis. "Who does that?"

"Everyone," the group replied. "You're a big liar. Who's next?"

"Who's number two?"

"Me," said Sally, "and I choose a truth." She reached into the hat of questions. "Okay, it reads, have you ever farted loudly in class? Oh, my God...well, I'll be honest, once I did in Spanish, and when everyone was looking around to see who it came from, I looked around too like it wasn't me! I was so mortified." She hid her face. I have to give it to Sally; I don't know if I would have admitted that in a group. Either brave or very stupid. I shook my head.

"Okay, number three, pick a truth or a dare," said Liz, moving across the room closer to where I was sitting.

"I'm gonna pick a dare," Jennifer said hesitantly. "Please don't make it too gross."

"Okay, said Liz, "Pretend you have a booger in your nose and try to pick it without using your finger."

"Hey, I said not too gross. That's really gross! All right..." Scrunching her nose up and down, she tried to wipe it on her shoulder, then sat down and tried to wipe it on her knee. Finally, to everyone's amazement, she pretended to try and pick it with her big toe. An award-winning performance for sure, and everyone was roaring with laughter.

"That's a hard act to follow, Jenn, but number four is up next. Truth or Dare?"

"I'm number four," replied Tessa, "I'll take a dare, but no way am I going to pretend to pick my nose!"

"Dare it is. Okay, I dare you to act like a drunk chicken."

With that, Tessa started roaming around the bedroom, scratching up sleeping bags with her feet, flapping her arms while walking wobbly, falling down then lying on her back with her feet up in the air and finally going to sleep while still snoring and clucking. She was great and everyone applauded. By now, I'd noticed that Liz was sitting next to me, still laughing from the drunken chicken impersonation.

"Next is number five," announced Liz. "Who's five?"

"I'm five," said Vicky. "I'll take a truth. I think it might be safer."

"The truth question is have you ever peed in a pool?"

"Oh, my gosh. Peed in a pool, yeah, probably when I was little, but not recently. Why would you do that, it's nasty! Who pees in a pool at our age?" she asked, scrunching up her face.

Numbers six and seven were boring and I was losing interest in the game, glad I was the last number to choose a truth or a dare. Trying to revive the lagging enthusiasm and laughter shown at the beginning of the game, I handed the number eight paper to Liz. Then I announced loudly, with my arm in the air, pretending to be a Shakespearian character giving a speech, "In honor of Liz's birthday, I will not only pick one dare, but I will also pick a second dare, so bring on your most embarrassing yet." I bowed exaggeratedly. Somewhere way in the back of my mind, I thought I might be setting myself up for some social discomfort by this announcement, but like most star-struck showoffs, I immediately dismissed that thought. I really wanted to impress Liz on her birthday, and I was sure this performance was going to be successful.

"Okay, you're sure you want two? 'Cause one's all that's required," replied Liz.

"Go for it, My Lady, announce my dares." I thought I was getting maybe a bit too far into character with the My Lady part, but everyone was laughing and it was fun to say it in an Ol' English accent.

"I've got one dare," said Mavis. "Show us how you make out using a mirror. Anyone have a hand mirror?"

What happened to the piss and B.O. questions? I thought, confused. Nobody asked any sexy dares. I don't want a dare pertaining to anything kinda like sex, I thought frantically. Make out with a mirror? Wow, I had no idea how to make out with anything, let alone with an audience watching. Embarrassed, and not wanting to look directly at Liz, I took the mirror from Mavis and began to kiss it like I thought humans probably kissed someone else human, kinda puckered and moving my lips slightly around the mirror.

"More tongue," I heard Tessa shout.

"Go girl," encouraged Vicky.

The other girls started chanting. "Go! Go! Go! Yeah, great job, Sexy Susie, you must've had some practice!"

"Well, it's hard to top that performance, but you still have one more to complete, so this is your final dare," stated Liz. "With the lights off, I dare you to kiss the hand of someone in the room like you'd kiss your boyfriend. Nobody will know who you kissed, so it won't be weird or anything, right?"

Still trying to slow my frantic heart rate down from the mirror event, I was supposed to kiss someone's hand like I kiss my boyfriend? Was it just me that thought that was kinda weird? Why did Liz bring up that dare? Before I had a chance to come up with a plan, the lights went off in the room. Sitting there frozen with fear, I felt someone's lips gently on my lips. They were the softest lips, and then her tongue gently flicked mine. The lights came back on, everyone was chattering about whom I had kissed, and I just smiled at Liz.

***

I fumbled through seventh grade remaining near the bottom of the proverbial food chain, like a minnow in a tank of hungry piranhas. I worked hard at not standing out in any way besides my height, and trying to be invisible along with all the other poor souls who had been tricked into believing junior high school was going to be fun and exciting. The school year dragged on, week by week. Spring seemed like it would never end, and the far-off summer vacation was the only oasis in my junior high desert.

I continued to talk with Liz on a regular basis, though getting to see each other in person was almost impossible because she lived so far away. Bancroft had a seventh grade end of the year dance that I didn't want to attend. Truth be told, no one invited me. I spent the evening at home in my room, listening to Beach Boys records, and talking to Liz on the phone.

Chapter Twenty-one

SEPTEMBER OF 1963 MEANT the beginning of eighth grade. At the start of the school year, I was hopeful that this year would be better than last. I hoped I'd fit in more, grow less, and figure out how to better navigate the social scene. As usual, the school nurse weighed and measured us, and I had now grown to five-feet-nine-inches. There wasn't as much ruckus in the hall that year, because thankfully some of the boys had started to grow so now I wasn't the only one who was over five-feet-six-inches.

Eighth grade also meant the opportunity to attend 'Friday Nighters,' a school dance from seven to nine p.m. once a month in the gym for eighth and ninth graders. For those of us in eighth grade, it was exciting because it was the first time we would get to go without parents, and we were excited for the first dance to arrive.

At the start of school, everyone was talking about what they were going to wear, who was going, and scrambling to buy a ticket for one dollar. The school decorating committee made the decorations; the dance always had a theme and ugly posters and crepe paper streamers were hung all over the gymnasium, tying to give the appearance of a festive evening.

Most of the ninth graders thought the dances were 'rank' and few went, so it ended up actually being an eighth grade dance. The popular ninth graders were already having weekend parties at kids houses with little or no supervision. They consumed alcohol and cigarettes, and the hot topic around school became who was going to be the first of the girls to succumb to sex and eventually get pregnant.

The chaperones at Friday Nighters were four of the cool teachers at school who were supposed to keep everything under control for the two-hour time frame. Miss Gregory taught ninth grade English. She was young, blond, pretty, and everyone's favorite teacher. Then there was Mr. Jansen, who was one of the boys' gym teachers. It was whispered he had a crush on Miss Gregory. They would even dance together, which further caused kids to insist they were having an affair. The other two teachers were usually Mr. Tomlin, who taught U.S. History, and the Home Economics teacher, Miss Adams. A refreshment table with punch and cookies was set up, and benches were placed for kids to hang out on. As usual, the boys sat on one side of the gym—the one with the food—and the girls sat on the other side. This was fine with me because I really just wanted to hang around the girls.

A ninth grader was the disk jockey and he played records on a record player. You could write down requests for songs, put them in a bowl, and the DJ would draw one and read off the song and dedication if there was one. At the first month's dance in October, with a Halloween theme, no one made a request because we had only been in school less than two months. The girls were shy about dancing and the boys were downright mortified. Some girls were still quite a bit taller than the boys, and so not too many requests were plucked from the bowl. Undaunted, the DJ played all the top forty hits and most of the dancing was between the girls. Not about to dance, I just hung out, teasing girls I liked, eating the refreshments, and wishing Liz was in the group.

***

In eighth grade, every student at Bancroft Junior High had to take a career test to help them assess areas of interests and possible career paths. It was called something like 'what you like to do and what you would be good at' testing. Students took it as a joke, though teachers tried to make us take it seriously. There were questions about what you liked to do and what kind of career would match those talents. Careers? We were barely ready to turn fourteen years old. What careers? I didn't know the kind of cereal I wanted for breakfast the next day, let alone what to be for the rest of my life.

Teachers gave the tests during Social Studies. "Fill in the bubbles completely, use a sharpened number two pencil, and the test will suggest your best career choice." The questions were something like this: Would you rather build a birdhouse or work at a swimming pool? Both sounded good to me. Do you like being alone or do you like to be with others? Who are the others, my parents or my friends? Do you like being outdoors or do you want to work in an office at a desk? Probably not the general office scenario for me. Do you like animals or cars? I have a dog and would like a car when I'm older. Which is the right answer?

Ninety-nine percent of the eighth graders half-heartedly filled in the blanks and wondered why anyone would ask those questions. The final question was "What would you most like to be when you grow up?" Thinking of the previous forest ranger and zookeeper questions, and thinking how funny it would be when the teacher read my answer, I wrote, "a frog." I should have already heard the sound of the counselor dialing my parent's telephone number regarding this answer by the time we passed the tests up to the front of the row.

"Your school counselor wants to meet with us regarding the results of your occupational testing," said my mother the following Monday, when I arrived home from school.

By the look on her face, I knew it was not because I did particularly well on the career test. "Okay," I said, shrugging nonchalantly.

"This is not a joke!" she informed me. "I am humiliated by your answer."

"Okay," I shrugged again.

"Did you write down that you wanted to be a frog?"

"What do ya mean?"

"Did you write down that you wanted to be a frog when you grow up?" Mom's voice rose multiple decibels and pronouncing each individual syllable like her audience was either hearing impaired or dense.

"What are ya talking about?" I retorted, annoyed, but knowing now what she was referring to.

"Listen to me, missy. The tests they gave you are important. It may be the answer to what you will be for the rest of your life. Being a frog is not a legitimate answer to the question," she said, and it was clear she was angry.

"So forest ranger is?" I asked. "What woman do we know who is a forest ranger? Ranger Rachel? The test was stupid, so I gave a stupid answer. What did you say when they asked you, a housewife? Huh, I don't know what I want to be, but I don't want to be a housewife and a mother. Maybe I will raise chickens," retreating to my bedroom.

Once again, we attended the parent/teacher/student conference with me teetering on the brink of prison, in my mother's (and certainly grandmother's) opinion. Martha Webb repeatedly apologized for my answers, while I daydreamed about what it would actually be like to raise chickens. The counselor spent a half an hour emphasizing to my mother how important vocational testing was to an eighth grader in relation to eventually having a job. Tapping at my answers and then pointing back at me, he repeatedly made his fears known that I was heading down the wrong path with my attitude of disrespect for this test. Further, he warned, students like me would only sink deeper in their insolent attitude if parents did not make it crystal clear to their children that they should reform their thoughts and attitudes immediately. My mother looked like a soldier who was being brainwashed and sent off to war. She sat up straight, listened intently, and with eyes wide, assured the counselor I would be changing my attitude within the hour.

I knew I was supposed to fall into the ranks of the reformed as we left his office. My mother charged off to battle, with me trying to catch up in double time. "Hurry up. Get into the car," she commanded to me. Once into the car, she glared at me with a cold, steady gaze. "I have never been so embarrassed in my life," she stated, emphasizing her embarrassment by speaking each syllable slowly. I was on restriction for the entire weekend, she informed me as we drove back home.

"Big deal," I said under my breath.

She slammed on the car brakes, and the car veered toward the right curb. "What did you say?" she demanded.

I had never seen her this angry with me and did not feel at all confident telling her what I had really said for fear she would actually slap me—hard. "Nothin'...I didn't say anything."

Breathing hard, she took her foot off the brake, hit the gas, and we lurched towards home in her seafoam green 1960 Ford Galaxy. My maternal grandmother, who was at the house when we got back, asked where we'd been.

"Susan had a problem with a test at school," replied my jailor.

"What test?" asked my grandmother, squinting and leaning towards my mom to hear the answer.

"A career test of some sorts. I really don't want to talk about it now, Mom."

"I told you there was something not right about that child, Martha."

Mom looked at my grandmother and back at me, but said nothing.

"She needs some kind of professional help; she's just not right," my grandmother continued, pointing towards me and shaking her head. "Just not right, never has been."

"Enough, Mother, please."

**

I continued my friendship with Liz on the phone and was completely devastated when she told me her family was moving to Oregon. Right before they moved, I rode my bike over twenty miles to her house. I was trying not to cry, as was Liz when she hugged me goodbye, assuring me she would continue to call and keep in touch. Totally crushed, I rode the twenty or so miles back, crying most of the way home.

I knew people meant well when they said they'd keep in touch, so there was a little hope, but deep down, I knew it probably wouldn't happen. In the emptiness I felt without Liz, it seemed like I would never feel that way again about someone. I moped around for a few weeks, feeling sorry for myself. Even my brain-dead brother noticed something was wrong.

"You okay?" Randy asked one morning. "You've been acting like someone died or something. I mean, Mom even asked me about it."

"I'm okay, no big deal. Like I'd tell you if something was wrong, so, what, you could make it worse?"

"Sorry for caring, you dork. I just wondered if you were okay, that's all. Forget it!"

"Just shut up, you jerk."

"You shut up, creep."

"No, you shut up!" By now, both of us were laughing and I did feel a little better.

Even though finally managing to figure out how to navigate junior high school more effectively, there were still moments of pure panic socially. Lunch was where I learned what the other girls were doing, wearing, and thinking. It's where the new fashion trend of stretch pants with stirrups first came up, and I learned everyone was getting some and wearing them on weekends to go to the movies or a party if you could get invited to one, so they immediately went on my radar also.

"Have you heard about stretch pants with stirrups?" I asked my mom. "Everyone's wearing them, so can I get a couple of pairs?"

"I don't see why not, they look cute on the TV," she replied.

Who cares if they wear them on the television? I liked them simply because they were a form of pants. Any kind of pants was better than a skirt or dress in my mind.

"Get some money out of my purse and you can go try them on at the MayCo. If they fit, you can get two pairs."

I phoned Vicky, and she agreed to go with me. Now that we were eighth graders, it was rank to ride bikes, so we planned on walking to the new shopping center on Saturday morning. We met at the halfway point and began the walk, talking about school stuff and the kids we liked and those we didn't.

"You ever hear from Liz?" she asked seriously.

"No. It's a long-distance call, so it's expensive. My mom said I couldn't call her."

"I know she misses you. She really liked you, Susan; she told me several times."

"Yeah, I miss her a lot. I haven't met anyone else like her. I wish I would."

"I know it's harder for you and Liz to find someone, but it'll happen, I just know," said Vicky.

"Yeah, I guess. Wish it would hurry up!" I said brightly, bumping my shoulder against Vicky's, grateful she was my friend.

Arriving at the shopping center, we headed for the MayCo. Passing up the girls' department and heading up the escalator to the women's, I walked towards the mannequins modeling the trendy stretching pants. I held up a black pair at my waist to see how long the legs would be before they stretched, and it was already evident the pants weren't long enough.

"Do they have longer ones?" asked Vicky. "Those look a little short."

"Everything looks a little short on me, if you hadn't noticed," I said. "I think they'll be okay. They're supposed to stretch." Pulling the pant legs like a stretch band across my chest. "See, they'll be fine."

We walked home to our halfway spot and parted ways. "See ya Monday at school," she said.

Happily, I continued to walk home, imagining the possibilities ahead in my new stretch pants, sure they would fit perfectly. Undressing, and then taking the blue pair out of the bag and slipping them on, I made sure the arch of my foot held the stirrup, then, pulling on the other leg, I stood up to pull the pants up to my waist. I could get them up to my waist if they were stretched to capacity, but then if I let go of the top of the pants, the waist would snap down to my mid-thighs. I unsuccessfully tried a few more times to stretch them up to my waist, but it was apparent there was no way the pants would stay at my hips unless I held them there. Crap. Maybe I should undo the stirrups. Taking my feet out of the bottom part of the pants, I pulled them up again to my waist. The waist stayed put this time, but the legs of the stretch pants were now midway between my ankles and my knees. They were no longer fashionable and trendy stretch pants, more like baggy and stretched out pedal pushers.

A few days later, my mom asked me why I wasn't wearing my new pants. I told her they were too short; even though they stretched, they wouldn't stretch as much as I needed them to fit my height.

"Give them to me," said my mom.

"Why? Do you know magic and you can make them longer?"

"No, but remember when I helped you make your nylons longer? I know a trick," she said and winked.

I did remember, along with a flood of other memories of things she tried to help me with that turned out to be personal disasters. The pants were useless to me now, so I gave them to her. Later in the day, I saw them hanging in the laundry room with good ol' Campbell's Chicken Soup cans inserted into the legs. Leave it to my mom. After she wet and stretched them, they actually did fit better, though it still looked a little like the crotch of the pants was drooping down towards my thighs.

***

By the time Bancroft's Winter Ball came, some of the short boys had grown an inch or so, kids had gotten to know each other, and there were some couples dancing. The DJ played a request or two, but none with dedications. By February, the Valentine's Dance was the talk of the eighth grade. Some kids were going steady and boys began to talk about having dates to the dance, though the school frowned upon students dating.

I'd gone to some of the school dances early on, but no one ever asked me to dance. I thought I might go to the Valentine's Dance, if my friends were going, but hadn't dreamed of going with anyone. As I arrived home from school, my mother announced, "Michael Green's mother called today, and he would like you to accompany him to the Valentine's Dance on Friday night. His mother will pick you up and then drive you and Michael to the dance and bring you home at the end."

"Michael Green—are you kidding? No way that's happenin', Mom."

"Why? The Greens are a nice family, Susan."

"I don't care how nice they are. I'm not going as Michael's date to any school function, or any other function for that matter. He has a million zits! No damn way! I don't even like him; he's weird," shaking my head.

"Watch your language, Susan."

"I'm not doing it, and you can't make me," hunkering down for a fight. "Besides, the school frowns upon kids our age dating, you know that," I said with an air of confidence.

"It's not a real date, Susan; it's just a way for both of you to go together."

"I don't need a way to go, Mom. I have a way to go. Dad drives me there." I was on the verge of tears. "Absolutely not!" I said as my voice got louder, heading towards my room and slamming the door. God. Michael Green...are you kidding me? What a dorky, zit-faced loser. Oh my God. Never! I don't know what was said between our mothers or how mine bowed out of the ridiculous idea, but she didn't mention it again to me.

I did go to the Valentine's Dance alone, drank a lot of punch, ate a lot of cookies, and as usual, didn't dance, but at least I had my pride. Michael came, wearing a green suit and tie that made him look like a leprechaun. His date, unattractive Lorie Hanson, looked like Mr. Ed the talking horse, with her huge toothy smile. Everyone was laughing and snickering at them, making horse sounds and talking about the pot of gold at the end of the rainbow, and I was grateful I hadn't given into another of my mother's stupid ideas. I had enough problems on my own.

Someone put a request into the DJ's bowl for the song by Jimmy Soul with the lyrics, "If you want to be happy for the rest of your life, never make a pretty woman your wife," with a dedication supposedly from Michael to Lorie. Then someone else put in a request for "Going to the Chapel" by the Dixie Cups, supposedly from the effeminate male cheerleader Casey Anderson to Grant Bryant, the star football quarterback. Total pandemonium broke out and the dedication bowl quickly disappeared.

I went to a few more of the dances and finally, by March, stopped going entirely. What was the point? The whole couple concept was outside my reality, so why bother? I'd rather stay home, eat raw chocolate chip cookie dough, and watch James Bond movies, imagining I saved the beautiful woman on the black and white TV in my room.

In May, school droned on with dumb homework and the end of the school projects loomed. I was terrible in math, marginal in history, Spanish, and English, strong in science and creative writing, and great in P.E., so while dreading any history or English projects, I knew I'd ace science and creative writing.

The science teacher, Mr. Coleman, announced our last weeks of school were going to be spent discussing dinosaurs and evolution. It sounded interesting; I liked archaeology and had read books about Lewis Leakey's digs in Africa. His wife, Mary, was also an archaeologist and paleoanthropologist, which I thought was a really cool job for a woman.

As interesting as Mr. Coleman's classroom discussions were, I sometimes daydreamed about a variety of topics, including which girl currently fascinated me. Imagining myself teasing and poking her, enjoying her reaction, I suddenly realized the teacher had just said the word homo in science class. Snapping back from my fantasy world, appalled when he said it again.

Next, he wrote Homo Erectus on the blackboard in big letters, and he continued on, saying, "Homo Erectus were the first species of early humans who began to evolve over 200,000 years ago in Africa." A few others in class looked confused, which isn't unusual in any eighth grade class, but no one looked as shocked as I would have thought, considering he just said and wrote the word Homo Erectus on the board. Was I the only one who was aghast our science teacher would blatantly talk about homos and erections in the classroom or did I miss something?

Now I was hyper alert as Mr. Coleman began to say kids' names in the classroom. "Mark is a Homo Sapiens as is Westley and your classmate, Susan."

Horrified, I shouted, "I am not a homosexual. That's a lie; I like boys just like all the other girls!" now shaking and blinking back tears. The class looked like I had just announced I was a mass murderer who preferred teenage victims from a science class.

The teacher must have realized what I thought he had said, because he quickly added, "I'm a Homo Sapiens too, class, all of us are. Homo Erectus are who we evolved from, so they're the earliest human beings."

Realizing my mistake, and regretting the outburst, I stared glumly my desk for the rest of the period, wishing I would just vanish.

After class, everyone seemed to pretend I didn't exist. No one walked with me, no one struck up a conversation, and no one said anything about what had just happened. Maybe I did vanish, I thought. Later in the day, a girl named Sheila tried to make me feel better by saying she wasn't paying attention either and also thought Mr. Coleman had said homosexual instead of homo sapiens.

"Yeah, but you didn't totally embarrass yourself by shouting out you weren't one and liked boys like I did. You had enough sense to keep your mouth shut," I said glumly.

"I'm not sure if it was having more sense," said Sheila. "It shouldn't matter if he did say homosexuals; there's nothing wrong with them. My uncle is homosexual. Well, he calls himself gay, and he's a really great guy. My mom says he was just born that way and there's nothing wrong with it. So even if you were one, and I'm not saying you are, it doesn't matter 'cause you're still okay just as you are. I gotta go. See you tomorrow."

I mulled that conversation around in my head for the next few hours; the words 'gay and born that way' were all new concepts to me. Am I gay? I thought again.

I did my final book report on the Leakeys and their discoveries in Africa and received an A minus from Mr. Coleman, which made me happy. He probably thought it best to stay positive around me since I apparently had difficulty hearing as well as a tendency to shout out strange things.

School was finally over in June, and summer began, ending another school year. I had learned to maneuver eighth grade marginally easier than seventh grade, but was grateful for three months away from all the stress. Trying to keep up with what to like, wear, or be was very stressful for those of us outside the in crowd. In addition, the height issue continued to plague me. Now five feet-eleven-inches, and still growing, the looming red line on the back of the door in my bedroom continued to taunt me. Measuring myself obsessively a few times a week, I tried to slump, re-measure, and slump again, willing the line measuring my height to stop moving upwards, but remained powerless over my body.

There was nothing particularly noteworthy about the summer of eighth grade except my brother gave me his old surfboard and I learned how to surf. I loved the ocean, the sun, and the surf, and I became a fair surfer over that summer. Of course, I was the only girl surfer at Seal Beach, but the boys seemed okay with me. While surfing, I fit in just a little more. It was a good summer. No one asked me to dance, no one cared how tall I was, and no one said what I should or shouldn't wear. All the boys at the beach wore jams. I wore a bikini top and jams and fit right in.

Chapter Twenty-two

STARTING NINTH GRADE WITH sun-bleached hair and a tan bolstered my self-esteem, finally feeling able to handle junior high school. Yeah, I was going be teased sometimes, but didn't have to take it to heart and wilt inside. I was starting not to care what kids said about me, and accordingly, the school tormentors seemed to lose interest. I was finally coming into my own, all five-feet-eleven-inches of me; the school nurse announced this loudly and clearly to everyone in the hall line the second week of September 1964. This time no one said anything.

The normal-sized kids remained normal-sized and Willy Hamilton, also called 'Pimple,' because he was small and had acne, finally had grown about an inch in the whole three years of junior high. I told him he should have changed his name to 'Boil' to celebrate the increase in his size, but he didn't think that was too funny. I could have gotten a lot of laughs for that observation, but I didn't want Willy to feel any worse than he was feeling about being so short, sympathetic for being on the opposite end of that scale.

Over the summer, the Woodle twins lost weight and blossomed into less identical, less overweight boys, and finally gave up matching shirts. William began to go by Bill, and Wesley by Wes, so just by using nicknames, they started to separate into two different boys in everyone's eyes. We were all in our final year of junior high and on the cusp of young adulthood and were getting more and more full of our perceived independence and ourselves.

Happily, for me, ninth grade breezed by. An average student, I had a quick crush on an older girl at my church, but no one made me feel like when I was with Liz. By the summer of 1965, I was fifteen years old, going to be a high school freshman in the fall, and I had a boyfriend named Rick.

When I look back on it, he was so gay. He had no physical expectations of me, and that was the reason we hung out. Rick was a sophomore in high school and knew my friend Walter, who liked my other friend Barbara. My mother continued to try and maintain a chokehold on my budding freedom by requiring me to come home from wherever by nine p.m. That summer we all hung out together, went to each other's houses, attended Elks Club dances, and generally had fun together, except I had to be home two hours earlier than everyone else.

Rick had his own 1948 grey primered Chevy we called the 'Rhinoceros.' He picked up Walter, and then they would come over to my house, park the car, and we'd walk to Barbara's house around the corner. I wasn't allowed to ride in Rick's car because my mom didn't think it looked safe. It actually was probably safer than some of the newer cars were, but there was no negotiating with her. No riding in Rick's car was the law. Barbara's dad would have to drive us to dances at the Elks Club, and I still had to be home by ten p.m., earlier than everyone else did. Those were the rules for that summer. Period.

The Elks Club dances were different from most teen dances in that they hired a live band for each dance and then charged four bucks for a ticket to get in. Lots of teenagers wanted to come, but Elks members purchased many of the tickets for friends and family, so the outside public who got to attend the dance was limited. Barbara's dad always bought ours, so we went to every dance, which made us feel kinda hip and cool even though we were in no way hip *or* cool.

Walter was big and heavy and wore bright colored shirts, I was tall, skinny, and athletic, Rick was effeminate, and Barbara, who was decades ahead of herself, dressed in all black like Morticia from the Addams Family. Barbara created and perfected the look before anyone had heard of dressing Goth. We were quite the foursome.

Once Sam Shatole, from our old junior high, showed up at the Elks dance. I guess he was lucky enough to be able to purchase one of the tickets, 'cause I'd never seen him there before. Sam was a giant bully and an asshole in my book. At Bancroft, he'd tormented all the unathletic boys, calling them queers, and instilled fear in any of us that might be questioning our sexual orientation. Once I ran into him in the hall in between classes and he walked in front of me, almost causing me to trip. "You're pretty clumsy for a jockette, better watch where you're going Lady Lesbo." I kept quiet even though I wanted to sock him in the mouth, as he meandered down the hall towards his next class.

As the next song started, my friends and I sprung out on the dance floor. I was actually a fairly decent dancer thanks in part to my pathetic Don's and Deb's participation, and now that my partner was equal in height, we bopped around the dance floor, showing off all our moves. Towards the end of the dance, we were standing by the refreshment table, talking and laughing, when Sam walked up.

"Well, look what we have here. It's Licky Ricky the fag and his girlfriend Lady Lesbo, along with Fat Walter and his girlfriend Black Barbie. What are you losers doing here?"

"Get lost, Sam," I said.

"Who's gonna make me?" he said, with an obvious smirk on his face.

"Just leave us alone, Sam," said Rick.

"Like I said, who's gonna make me, Lady Lesbo or her boyfriend, Licky Ricky the fag?"

Before I knew what happened, I shoved Sam Shithole backwards, knocking him into the wall, awkwardly bending my right wrist.

"I guess Lady Lesbo, Sammy boy. Now shut the hell up and leave us alone."

Sam steadied himself and quickly walked away, disappearing into the crowd.

"Damn, that was great! Weren't you afraid?" asked Barbara.

"Afraid of what? It dawned on me. He's never gonna tell anyone he got shoved into the wall by a girl. What guy would admit to that, so what did I have to lose? This is the second time he's called me Lady Lesbo just to piss me off, so I figured he had it coming. The first time he bugged me at school, I was afraid of what he could do to embarrass me. Now I realize he's not gonna say anything." I grinned.

"How's your wrist?" asked Walter.

"It actually hurts a lot more than they show in the movies," I said, rubbing the wrist with my left hand, "but I'm okay. It felt good to shove him. Let's dance some more."

"You can defend me anytime." Walter laughed.

"Us too!" Said the rest of our group.

***

When I first met Rick, he told me his mom had been paralyzed in a car accident, so I knew she used a wheelchair. Eventually, when I met his mother, I thought she was really cool. She was divorced and more like a friend than a parent. She would let her kids sit in their family room, watch TV, and neck with their dates, while she drank beer and smoked cigarettes. Rick and I never kissed for fairly obvious reasons, but the other kids took advantage of the opportunity as often as it was presented.

During that summer, Rick's mom would frequently offer to take everyone to the beach at night for beach parties, but I could never go. They would have bonfires, eat junk food, and I was dying to go along, but knew my folks would say, "No way." They'd never let me even associate with the family if they knew his mom drank beer while our friends necked.

I was also sure if my mom knew his mom was paralyzed it would have been the end of my visits to his house. To my mother's odd way of thinking, handicapped people needed to get their rest and didn't need to be dealing with a bunch of hormonal teenagers. I never really understood my mom's theory regarding handicapped individuals needing more rest, but I assumed she got it from her own mother.

When Rick's mom would pull up in front of our house to get me, I'd shout good-bye and quickly leave before my mom could ever see anything but Rick's mom waving from the car. That way she always looked just friendly and not actually crippled. Rick said since his mom was paralyzed, she had their station wagon outfitted with controls that allowed her to drive and maneuver the car brakes with her hands. However, she couldn't get out of the car without using a wheelchair.

Each week, Walter, Barbara, Rick, his sister, and her boyfriend would all beg me to come for the beach party. In my mind, it was impossible. My parents would never agree to such a plan, and I knew they'd kill me if they found out I'd gone without telling them. Finally, while hanging out one evening, their tales of past beach parties got the better of me. I relented, and off we all went for a beach party. I was giddy with deception and freedom, and with no remorse, that I'd just lied to my parents. By God, I was going to a beach party! My nine p.m. curfew seemed days away as we zoomed past Surfside Beach, careening towards the series of events that would unfold in Huntington Beach.

At the place on the beach known as The Cliffs, Rick's mom began to drive a little wobbly. No one else seemed to notice, so I tried to ignore the periodic drifting over the yellow line since his mom often drove a little wobbly. I never knew if she had been drinking or if it was because she was driving and braking with only her hands. She lost control of her state-of-the-art, modified station wagon when she swerved to avoid something in the road, and suddenly the car went airborne, heading towards the beach, coming to a stop some ten feet off the road, lodging in the sand.

Oh, shit, I thought, this is bad. Everyone but Rick's mom got out of the car and stared at the tires stuck in the sand. No one knew what to do, so I took control. We took all the things out of the back of the wagon and looked for tools, but there were none. Since I was the only one with a looming curfew, I instructed everyone to find boards, bushes, trash, rocks, or whatever they could find to put under the back tires of the car for traction, having seen my dad do this many times when we got stuck in the sand on dirt roads. In the frenzy that followed and now in complete darkness, somehow my beach towel and t-shirt also got thrown under the tires. The tires spun around wildly but the station wagon didn't move an inch. Suddenly, realizing my shirt and towel where under the tires and were now shredded, black, and stunk like burning rubber, all I could think again was, "oh, shit."

After discussing our options, or actually our lack of options, we finally decided four of us would hitchhike to the nearest town to call for a tow truck, while Rick's sister and her boyfriend would stay behind with her mom. Four teenagers hitchhiking in the dark at nine o'clock in the evening on Pacific Coast Highway stood out like a giant sore thumb. No sympathetic car stopped, only a Huntington Beach police officer. He drove us to town, where we called a tow truck and then drove us back to the car. I was a nervous wreck that the officer would conclude Rick's mom had been drinking, arrest her, and I'd have to call my parents from the Huntington Beach jail. Fortunately for me, he didn't.

We got home very late. My mother was still up waiting for me and she was furious. I made up some lame excuse for being so late, saying Rick's mom's car broke down and I couldn't find a phone to call home. My mother, with eyes narrowed, surmised I was lying, since there was nowhere in the civilized world I couldn't have found a pay phone to call home if I'd tried. Immediately she cut off my relationship with Rick, saying he was too old and had way too many privileges. My smelly, tattered clothes ended up in our trashcan along with most of my freedom.

Chapter Twenty-three

SINCE RICK AND HIS family were off my approved social list, I started spending more time with a friend from school named Shelly McEllis. Shelly and I had known each other throughout junior high and sometimes hung out together. She was blindingly white-skinned, freckled, and could never manage to tan no matter how she tried, but she was funny and I enjoyed her company. She was in the outcaste group too.

Shelly had fat chubby legs that looked like pegs, large thighs at the top and skinny little ankles at the bottom. In addition, she had red frizzy hair that bounced as she walked. I would burst out laughing when I'd see her walking because her hair literally bounced up and down, like a giant oversized clown wig.

Shelly was the product of a second marriage. Her older half-sister, Sharon, was already in community college and drove a shiny new Volkswagen Beetle. Sharon would zoom us around town and we loved that she didn't shun us like older siblings did. Randy would never have been so friendly. Sharon even tried to teach me to drive her VW stick shift in the parking lot of the MayCo, though I could never seem to master the clutch and the gas pedal at the same time. She was just so nice to us, and we loved her for it. When we were with her, our lives seemed to be good, however brief the period of time. How we repaid Sharon for her kindness and acceptance went like this.

I had spent the night at Shelly's house on Saturday night many times because her mom and step-dad went out every Saturday night to eat, drink, and play cards with their friends. On this Saturday, my dad dropped me off at about seven p.m. to spend the night. Sharon had left earlier with a group of her friends, so there we were, ready for a boring night of TV, coke, and popcorn. That was before I discovered there was a very large jug of red wine under Shelly's mother's kitchen sink.

"Who drinks that?" I asked.

"My mom and step-dad."

"What does it taste like?"

"I dunno. I never tasted it."

I grabbed a large juice glass from the cupboard and filled it to the brim with red wine. Taking a deep gulp, I retched at the taste.

"Oh my God! It's really sour! Do you have any sugar?"

"Yeah, here," said Shelly, adding sugar and stirring with a spoon.

I took another swig. "Ugh, it still tastes really bad."

"Just drink some and give it to me."

I gulped and swallowed, thrusting the glass in her direction. "It's your turn," I said, grimacing, barely able to swallow, as Shelly took two big gulps while pinching her nostrils closed.

"Oh my God," she said, her freckled face all puckered up. "Why do they drink this shit?" She thrust the glass back in my direction. We each drank another, bigger swig and finished the glass.

This was the first time I had ever tasted alcohol, and I didn't know what to expect. I thought I might become a slobbering drunk, like I'd seen on TV. Instead, I just felt a little strange and uncertain. We kept looking at each other for the signs of intoxication, but no falling down and no slobbering transpired.

"What do you wanna do?" asked Shelly. "Watch TV?"

"No," I replied, "let's go for a ride in your sister's VW."

"What?" said Shelly. "Neither one of us knows how to drive a stick."

"I do," I replied casually. "Remember, she taught me in the MayCo parking lot."

"No, you don't, you couldn't do it," Shelly reminded me.

"Yes, I did. Come on, get her keys," I said feeling confident.

We got into Sharon's car, which was parked in the driveway. Depressing the clutch, putting the Bug in neutral, and turning the key, just like Sharon showed me, only produced a 'grumble, grumble, grumble' as the engine sputtered and died. Pumping the gas again, I revved the engine, trying to keep the car running.

"Shh, someone will hear us," Shelly warned.

"They'll just think it's Sharon leaving to go somewhere," I said. "She always goes out on Saturday nights. This is normal."

Normal, when you just had a glass of red wine laced with sugar, takes on a new meaning. Next, I tried to get the car into reverse over the loud complaints of the gearbox.

"You're gonna wreck her car!" warned Shelly.

"Shut up, no I'm not. I just can't find reverse in the dark," I answered over the grind of the transmission for a second time.

"Where are the lights?" I asked.

"What lights?" answered Shelly.

"The dome lights, you idiot, so I can find reverse gear."

"I dunno..." Shelly said, her voice fading. "Stop! Just turn it off. Sharon is gonna kill me. Plus I don't feel too good."

"What do ya mean, you don't feel very good?" I asked, right before Shelly vomited a dark stream of vile smelling red wine and sugar onto her lap.

"Oh my God," she blurted out, as she heaved again. The putrid smell of the vomit sent me into the dry heaves, and then, shortly after, into the real thing. Unlike Shelly, I managed to hurl the sugary red wine outside of the car instead of inside on my lap. Now we had managed to vomit both inside and on the side of Sharon's shiny beige VW without even leaving their driveway. Crap, I thought, this wasn't a very good idea. We should've watched movies.

By the time Shelly's mom and step-dad returned home from dinner, drinks, and cards, we had filled the wine bottle to its previous level with water, cleaned up Sharon's car with diluted Pine Sol, washed and dried a load of our vomit drenched laundry, and retreated to bed. The room continued to spin until we fell into a fitful, sweaty sleep. First drunk, first joy ride. Neither one was very much fun.

Shelly's older step-brother, Mike, was married and had two kids of his own who were just a few years younger than Shelly and I. Shelly's mother somehow convinced my parents that Mike was an upstanding family man who would never let us out of sight and they let me go with his family to water ski at the Colorado River. He and his friends owned expensive water ski boats and a large lot at the river's edge, where their families would go camping and water skiing every weekend in the summer.

The truth was, the adults would all get drunk, and the kids, varying in age from five to fifteen, would run amok with absolutely no supervision until the wee hours of the morning. This didn't seem strange to me however, because every group of adults camping around us was also drunk and their kids were running amok too. It was just one big, loud party starting on Friday night and lasting until Sunday morning.

During the days, we'd sit in the sun, water ski, and help on the docks. Sometimes Mike would even let me steer the boat, which made me feel grown up. We hooked up our rafts to the ski boat, skipping down the river, holding on for our lives as we bumped and sailed behind the boat. Occasionally, I would take my surfboard to the river and ride the wake created by the boat. In the early summer, we began skiing on two skis, and quickly progressed to a single ski. We learned how to jump the wakes and had an amazing time every minute we were there.

Though it was always one hundred and twelve degrees, we could cool off in the river or sit in the shade. Our sunburned noses were in a constant state of peeling, but we continued to tan and look healthy. However, Shelly, who alternated between lily white and lobster red, looked more like a lizard constantly molting its old skin. She couldn't get a tan, or even a beige, no matter what she did. At night, her white skin glowed in the moonlight and in the day, she fried from the sun, which pretty much made her skin match her hair color.

In the evenings, we found an array of things to entertain ourselves. The kids would play pranks on each other and run screaming into the desert night to hide. Kids stole beer from their parent's coolers and everyone would share the drinks. The older boys would swear they were drunk and would ride their bikes down the hill, onto a makeshift ramp, then sail up and then backdown crashing into the river, showing off for all the girls and younger kids.

Shelly's stepbrother and his wife were friends with another couple who usually came camping with us at the river. Their names were Tam and Larry. Tam was the most beautiful woman I thought I'd ever seen. She was tall, dark skinned, and had an incredible body in her tiny bikini. She was a great water skier and men migrated to our campsite just to check her out.

Her husband Larry drank too much and ended up acting like a jerk to her every time we were there, which made Tam really sad. Eventually fed up with his behavior, she'd take off into the desert just to get away from him and then return later, hoping he'd sobered up, but he never had.

Once in the late afternoon, all the kids were playing Hide 'n' Seek, and while looking for a hiding spot, I came across Tam sitting on a rock, crying. I didn't know if I should sneak off so she wouldn't know I saw her or if I should try to help her, but before I had a chance to decide, she looked up and saw me.

"Are you okay?" I asked, not knowing what to say.

"Yeah, I'm okay. I just hate it when Larry acts like such an idiot."

"Yeah, I feel sorry for you when he does that," I said, nodding my head slowly.

After a long silence, Tam turned and looked straight at me, putting her hand on my arm. "You know, when you're young, you don't realize how the decisions you make will affect your life later. I met Larry when I was eighteen, and he seemed to be the perfect guy; at least, that's what my friends and my parents thought. He was handsome and his family was rich, but he drank too much even then, and I knew he wasn't the right one for me.

"I really never wanted to marry him. I wanted to stay single, go to college, and maybe travel. In fact, I wasn't really sure I wanted to get married at all, but I gave in to everyone else's opinion. Now here it is twenty years later and I'm miserable. Take my advice, Susan. Don't settle for less than you deserve. Whomever you decide you love, make sure it's for the correct reasons. Don't listen to anyone who says you should choose one way or the other. Make sure you fall in love with the right person for you, not because anyone says you should."

I felt bad sitting there looking at her while she poured her heart out to me, especially since I listened to most of her speech while admiring how attractive her breasts looked in the fading light of the sunset. I assured her I would make the right choice when I finally fell in love. As she headed back to the campground and her jerky husband, I was glad to be only fifteen, and not facing any difficult decisions at that moment.

Another weekend, we were there with Mike and his family, and another family with two older teenage boys named Eddie and Frankie Lozario showed up to camp. On Saturday afternoon, after water skiing and hanging out all day, the boys quietly mentioned to Shelly and me they were going to steal their Uncle Carmine's ski boat later that night. They whispered they were secretly going to drive around the cove, and invited Shelly and me to come along for the ride. I thought it was strange they invited us because we were just going into high school, not attractive, and still flat chested, but they did and we accepted.

After dinner, while all the adults were drinking around fire pits, we vanished into the night to undock their uncle Carmine's boat and go joyriding. When the guys got the boat far enough out in the river where no one would hear, they gunned the engine and off we went. We went around the cove a few times and with each lap, Frankie drove the boat faster and faster. Shelly and I were in the back of the boat and Frankie and Eddie were in the front. They were talking, but the sound of the engine was so loud where we were sitting, you couldn't hear anything they were saying. The cove apparently got boring because the next thing I knew we were heading out to the open lake.

It was an unbelievably windy night outside of the cove on the open water. So windy there were large white capped waves, making for a very uncomfortable and jarring ride. Each time the boat hit a swell, it would become airborne and then slap down hard on the lake, sounding like it was going to break into pieces. In addition, each time the boat landed, I would bang my back against the inside of the boat.

Mr. Toad's Wild Ride went on until we were screaming at the boys to stop and take us back to camp. Laughing, they relented and drove us back to our campground. Approaching the dock as they were trying to park, they actually hit it, causing a noticeable ding in the hull. Shelly and I took off running so no one would know we'd been in the boat. With Shelly's little white peg legs glowing in the dark, we ran back towards camp through the bushes, managing to walk back into camp nonchalantly. Well, kinda nonchalantly. Shelly had bits of the bushes stuck in her big hair, but no one was paying any attention.

Sunday morning dawned hot. We got up, put on our bathing suits, and joined the rest of the families who were eating breakfast at a long wooden picnic table. The adults were hung over as always, already drinking the hair of the dog that had bitten them. Kids were arguing over cereal choices and suntan lotion was being applied heavily to all body parts exposed to the sun. On Sundays, we usually stayed until about noon before packing up and heading home. That meant we had about four hours of skiing and sun left that morning.

I was hunched over the table eating my cereal when I heard Mike's wife, Margie, say, "Oh my God, look at her back!" It took a second for me to realize that she was referring to me, as the little kids were jumping up and down, pointing at my back, and squealing. By now, I was standing up and trying to turn around to see my own back when Mike and some other men came up to see what the commotion was all about.

"Jesus," said Mike, "did an elephant give you that hickey?" All the kids laughed. I was still trying to see my back in a reflection from a car window and there was indeed a huge circular dark bruise on my lower right back, exactly where it was hitting the boat during our joyride with Frankie and Eddie.

"How did that happen, Susan?" questioned Margie with a concerned look on her face.

"I have no idea," I responded innocently, shrugging my shoulders.

"How can you have no idea how you got a bruise that big on your back? Does it hurt?" she said, pushing on it.

"Well, yeah, if you mash on it." The younger kids were now all making kissing and elephant trunk sounds, dancing around like a tribe of monkeys. "I'm fine," I said, trying to get the focus off of me and onto something else. Then we heard a commotion on the boat dock.

"What the hell happened to my boat?" a male voice could be heard asking loudly. "There's a God damn crack in the hull! Frankie! Eddie! You two know anything about this? I swear to God. If you two had anything to do with this, I'm gonna kill you dead," he said, slapping each boy hard on the back of his head as we all swarmed the dock.

This yelling definitely took focus off my bruised back, and put it on someone else. But by now, with Uncle Carmine yelling at the boys, I was sure they were going to confess and we would all get in trouble. Shelly and I quietly slipped away from the dock, as Carmine Lozario continued to alternately question, then smack Frankie and Eddie when he didn't like their answers. Neither one of the boys confessed, though I know Carmine thought they were both involved somehow."

All the way home from the river, Shelly and I would look at each other and break into uncontrollable giggles, slapping each other in the head, mimicking Uncle Carmine hitting Frankie and Eddie.

That summer was one of my favorites. Things were going well, I had friends, more freedom, and I was actually looking forward to September and the beginning of high school.

Chapter Twenty-four

CHANGE IS NEVER EASY, even when you're just moving from junior high up to high school. It took much of the last three years for me to get used to lockers, combination locks, and changing classes and now here we were again with new lockers, combinations, different school rules, and three thousand kids to contend with. It was overwhelming.

One week into tenth grade, the football team's schedule, football players, cheerleaders, and the pep squad became the only thing kids were talking about. Apparently high school football and its atomic bomb cloud of enthusiastic support overtook everyone at Lakewood High School, and every other high school in our district league.

That week, there were lunchtime pep rallies, and posters cheering on our team plastered on every empty space of every building both inside and outside the halls, including the chain link fences around the campus. Our band practiced their half-time show every lunch period and the team ran plays before school and then after until sundown. The football team wore their jerseys all week and there was no way Lakewood High School's Lancers were going to lose their first game of the season. At least, if it was up to our mascot Sir Lancelot, the pep squad, football team, and the cheerleaders.

Our school mascot wore an oversized white knight costume with a big red "L" on the front of the chest. A mask covered his face and the costume included a large metal lance and a shield, both used to hype up the crowd at rallies and games. The identity of the school mascot was supposed to always be a heavily guarded secret, which, if revealed, involved missing digits, a firing squad, or feet encased in cement. Basically, if anyone ever revealed the mascot's identity, they'd be scorned for their remaining years in school.

High school seemed so extreme compared to junior high school. Everything was much bigger, louder, more colorful, and much more exciting—and I'm just talking about lunch period. It really was fun to be part of such a large group. We were the Lakewood Lancers and we were winners.

By Friday morning, everyone was talking about that evening's game. It was a home game, which made it even better. Vicky, Shelly, and I decided to go together. Shelly's sister Sharon said she'd pick us up and drop us off, and Vicky's mom said she'd then pick us up after the game and take us all home. It sounded great to me, since my parents were completely uninvolved, and I could actually have a good time.

The game started at seven so Sharon picked me up, then we picked up Vicky and were at the football field by a quarter to seven. After proudly showing our Lakewood High School I.D. badges, we paid the one-dollar entrance fee, followed the crowd to the bleachers, and found empty seats. Seeing a few familiar faces, we smiled and waved, and waited for the activities to begin, so excited to be at our very first high school football game

The energy of the crowd was electric, and it surged into waves of clapping and feet stomping that the cheerleaders, who had assembled along with the pep squad in front of our side of the bleachers, led. Sir Lancelot was also there, waving his lance and shield, encouraging everyone to stomp, clap, and cheer. Every person in the crowd seemed to have on at least one red item of clothing, since it was our school color, and between red sweatshirts and red lettermen's jackets, it was obvious which side of the bleachers the Lancers claimed. Since it was a home game, we were squished to capacity. I knew a little about our high school players because our school newspaper had recently run an article on each guy, including an article on our mascot, Sir Lancelot.

"I thought no one knew who the person in the mascot suit was," quipped Shelly. "So how could they interview him? Did it come in the mascot uniform to be interviewed?"

"I heard it was Vic Cappy," I said.

"Didn't Crappy Vic go to junior high with us? Wasn't he in theater when they all acted out famous pictures in that one production and he portrayed the character in the painting American Gothic holding a pitchfork?" asked Vicky.

"Yup, that's him," confirmed Shelly

"He's Sir Lancelot?" I said. "Wow."

"He's weird. I saw him go after a kid with that pitchfork because the kid was bothering him, and he kept sticking the kid in the butt with the prongs while the kid screamed and tried to run away," said Shelly.

"Yeah, my recollection is that Crappy Vic gets annoyed really easily if anyone teases him," I recalled.

"Well, hopefully nobody will bother him tonight," said Shelly, just as the kickoff brought everyone to their feet while a huge cheer erupted in the bleachers, with shouts of, "Go Lancers!"

Our team honestly looked like they should have practiced at least a few more weeks, if not actually months, before they played their opening game. They dropped passes, missed throws, and even fumbled a hiked ball. Not what the hometown crowd was expecting by any means. The crowd's enthusiasm was beginning to turn from excited and cheerful to annoyed and grumbling as the seconds ticked on towards half time.

"They're not very good, are they?" Shelly giggled. "I was hoping for some touchdowns."

"You mean for our team and not just theirs?" I replied.

"Yeah, but I think you have to have the ball in your arm when you go over the end line. Not just run into the end zone for the heck of it," said Shelly.

"Most of the play seems to be at the other end of the field. Maybe when we switch goals our team will be where the action is," offered Vicky.

"I'm guessing no," I said, "based on how our team is playing. But let's keep hoping!" Mercifully, the first half ended with the score thirty-seven to zero.

Our half time show included one routine where the cheerleaders launched the smallest cheerleader into the air and the pep squad boys Casey and Andy were supposed to catch her. For some reason, after the girl was thrown up into the air, Casey and Andy moved the wrong direction to catch her and the poor girl came crashing down onto the heads of the other cheerleaders, who stumbled into our mascot, causing everyone to fall down into a large pile.

It's apparently hard to get up from lying flat on your back on the ground to a standing position when you're in a giant knight's costume with a lance and a shield. By the time they got Sir Lancelot upright again, it was obvious he wasn't happy by the way he stomped around the carnage. Throughout all of the confusion, the school staff tried to keep everyone in the bleachers off the football field, so the emergency responders could take three of the cheerleaders to the hospital to be checked out. All of this chaos took so much extra time, the second half started late, and everyone was beginning to get antsy and annoyed, including Sir Lancelot.

During the next play, a player from the other team ran out of bounds right where the remainder of our cheerleaders and pep squad were doing their cheers and acrobatics. He almost ran over Sir Lancelot, and as he was walking back onto the field, the mascot pretended to stick the other team's player in the back with his lance. This brought roars of cheers from our side of the bleachers and jeers from the other team's side, which just spurred the giant lancer on. Anytime one of the opposing team's players came close to the sideline, Lancelot would pretend to stab them with his lance, shaking his shield at them, and strutting back to the sideline before the next play. While this was uproariously funny to our team and crowd, it was significantly less funny to the opposing team and their supporters.

As the game continued and we actually began to score some touchdowns, our school mascot got increasingly emboldened in his antics. He'd run out onto the field in between plays and stab at the ankles of the other team, and he pretended to stab them in their butts. He even mimed stabbing one opposing player in the balls with his lance and then pantomimed hilarious laughter at the kid while holding his own baggy costumed crotch.

The school principal had enough and tried to physically restrain Sir Lancelot, but he got away, ran onto the playing field, and two of the opposite team players tackled him. As he hit the ground, the mascot's head flew off and rolled around on the third yard line. He slowly got up and started to try to really stab the players with his lance. The other players had to grab onto the metal spear so it wouldn't pierce them. Now it looked more as if they were playing tug o' war with the weapon, as football helmets came flying off and players began to take sides, trying to pull the lance away from the other team.

Security, team coaches, and school staff finally succeeded in getting the spear away from the players, but not before four people, including Sir Lancelot, actually received minor stab wounds to their torsos. The game was called early, and the dance that was supposed to be after the game in the gymnasium was cancelled for safety reasons and time to initiate a police investigation.

"Wow, do you think all the football games are this intense?" wondered Vicki.

"I don't know. I have nothing to compare it to, but I doubt it," said Shelly

"There's no way this is a normal game. What mascot tries to stab opposing players?" I said.

"I just know Crappy Vic is the mascot. Did you see how he wigged out and went after the other team's player? That's the same thing he did in junior high with the pitchfork," recalled Shelly. "I'm guessing he's not gonna be our mascot come Monday morning. He's too much of a liability—literally."

"Well, that was quite the first game of our high school experience. Our mascot tries to kill players on the opposing team with his Lakewood High School lance. Bet that makes the paper," I said.

Chapter Twenty-five

AFTER THE EXCITEMENT OF our first football game, we settled down into our routines of school, after school activities, homework, and our social lives. I tried out for the girls' swim team and made junior varsity. We worked out three afternoons a week after school and had swim meets on Thursdays. Girls' sports didn't get much publicity in those days, so there wasn't the pressure to win big and we all just had a lot of fun and made good friends.

One of my teammates was Cathy Dodd. She was on the varsity team. I knew her from Bancroft and she was an excellent swimmer, very strong and competitive having come from a private swim club background. Cathy had been teased in junior high school because she had short greenish-blond chlorine tinted hair and because they said she looked like a man—and she did. We were friends because we had the same interests, and besides that, she did look different than most of the girls, but I didn't really care what kids said about her.

I had occasionally swam on a club team in elementary school, but unlike her, I was never committed enough to do well. Ribbons and trophies literally covered her room and her family had their own swimming pool in their backyard. I enjoyed swimming and only won because I was taller than every other kid and my arms were longer.

Cathy was a swimming machine. She always won her events, which included backstroke, butterfly, and breaststroke. She wasn't as tall as I was, but had a much heavier build, with broad shoulders that tapered down to a thin waist. Her physique looked like she worked out with barbells; she was the only girl who could beat me at arm wrestling and she did it with little effort. I swam freestyle, so we didn't race against each other, which was fortunate because she could have easily beaten me.

A month into school and swim practice, Cathy asked me to a swim party at her house on a Saturday night with some of her swim club teammates. It sounded fun so I told her I'd come if I could get a ride. Asking my mother for permission to attend a party always caused me problems in junior high school because of it turning into an inquisition, and the trend continued in high school.

"Whose house?" asked my mom.

"Cathy Dodd. You know her and her mom; I've been invited to swim there before."

"What are the hours? Who's chaperoning?"

"From seven to eleven on Saturday night. You've met her mom before, and she'll be there, probably drunk and passed out with a joint," I answered in jest.

"What did you say? Drinking and passing out? Who?" My mom asked, frowning.

"Nothing. Her mom will be there. It's no big deal, Mom. For crying out loud. Why do you always do this to me? It's just a swim party, not a drug happening. I should just sneak out and go like most teenagers would, but no, I ask and I get to listen to you go on and on."

"I just want to make sure you're supervised, Susan. Call me a bad parent for caring."

"You're a bad parent for caring, Mom," I answered and smiled.

"Go away, you're bothering me," she said. "You can go."

***

You don't need to take much to a pool party. A bikini, a towel, and a comb should cover it. I arrived along with a trickle of other girls from Cathy's club team, none I knew. Cathy greeted us at the door and everyone was told to change into their suits and head for the pool. There was music playing and the pool was full with about a dozen teenage girls talking and screaming.

As it got dark, someone turned off the lights in the pool and we began to play Marco Polo. The next thing I knew, girls were taking off their bathing suits and tossing them on the deck of the pool. I'd never been anywhere where anyone took off their suits during a swim party, so I didn't know what to do. Should I leave mine on, making it obvious I was new to the group, or do what everyone else was doing and strip down? Going with the crowd seemed like the best idea, so off came my suit and I tossed it up on the pool deck along with everyone else's. I moved into deeper water so when I stood up the water came up to my neck. No way was I going to stand in the shallow end of the pool with my tiny boobs exposed for everyone to see.

"Isn't this cool?" asked a girl as she swam by. "It feels so natural to be naked." She was now floating on her back with her breasts and pubic hair glistening in the moonlight.

Natural was the opposite of what I was feeling at that particular moment; more like a pervert, since everyone in the pool had disrobed, and there was nowhere to look that didn't have a naked teenage girl in full view. Cathy swam up beside me, her large breasts bobbing in the water.

"What do ya think?"

"About what?" I said.

"All the girls being naked."

"Well, ah, I guess it's okay. Do you always do this at your parties?"

"Pretty much. Swimming naked is just relaxing, right?" said Cathy.

"Yeah, I'm definitely feeling something," I agreed, though relaxed would not have been the word I would have used to describe the feeling.

"Does it make you uncomfortable being around naked girls?" asked Cathy.

"Not uncomfortable necessarily, but awkward. I just wasn't expecting everyone to take off their suits and continue swimming. I've never been to a swim party before where anyone got naked," I replied honestly.

"You'll have to hang around with us more; I think you'd be pretty surprised by what goes on at our parties," said Cathy as she swam away.

At that moment, I was afraid to ask what else they did that would surprise me because this was already pretty surprising, and I wasn't sure I could handle anything bigger. Girls started getting out of the pool; some wrapped up in towels and some just dried off and continued to walk around the patio naked. Someone turned the music up and the dancing began.

My current focus was how to exit the pool and get to my towel with the minimal amount of exposure, but this was made much more difficult because now there were naked girls dancing and gyrating all over the pool deck and patio to the blaring music. I finally just got out of the pool, went straight to my towel, and wrapped it tightly around me, relieved to be safe and covered. A second later, Cathy, holding a bottle of beer in one hand, grabbed my towel with the other hand and yanked it off me to the cheers and laughter of the other girls.

"Come on, join the crowd," shouted one girl, as she did the shimmy.

"Be free!" shouted another, dancing around me like some May Day

Pole dancer, as her partner did some exaggerated rendition of a belly dance.

Oh, my God. Okay, now we were way outside of my comfort zone. I wasn't feeling particularly free, more like freaked out and wanting to run home.

"You seem kinda uptight," said a girl as she walked up beside me. "Here, have some of this." She handed me a bottle of beer. "It'll loosen you up."

"Where'd you get a beer? Isn't Cathy's mom home?" I asked.

"Does it look like Cathy's mom's home with all of us naked and drinking?" She said, laughing aloud, while swaying to the music. "Wanna dance?" When I didn't respond, she danced off towards another girl.

I made my way over to Cathy, who was standing by a cooler of beer. "Want one?"

"No thanks."

"How about a sip?"

"Okay." I took a drink from the bottle. "I thought your mom was going to be here tonight."

"No way, she'd never let us do this stuff if she was here. She'd freak out if she saw us naked and dancing."

"You told me earlier that I'd be pretty surprised to see what you all do at your parties. What did ya mean by that?"

"Well, let's just say this. We never invite boys and we have a lot of fun together. If you come back again, you'll see what I mean. Another sip?" She handed me the bottle and walked away. About ten minutes later, Cathy turned down the music and announced, "It's ten o'clock so remember, party's over at eleven."

It was starting to get cold, so girls began to put their clothes back on. When the music came on again, I noticed it had changed from rock and roll to a softer and slower type of music and girls began to slow dance together. I didn't want to stare, but I was fascinated watching two girls dancing slowly together. It seemed so gentle and sensual, and I was transfixed. A tap on my shoulder brought me back to reality when the same girl asked me to dance for a second time.

"I'm gonna really feel badly if you turn me down again," she said, smiling. "My name is Stacy. What's yours?"

"I don't really know how to dance slowly very well. Susan."

"My name is Stacy, not Susan."

"I know. I'm Susan. I just got nervous and I ran the two sentences together. Sorry."

"No problem. Stacy will now teach Susan to slow dance. Ready?" she said, taking my hand.

"Yup," I said, though I was so nervous. Then she put her arm around my shoulder and we began to dance slowly, body to body.

***

At swim practice on Monday, Cathy walked directly over to me and asked how I'd liked her party. I told her I'd never done anything like that before, but that I had fun and would like her to invite me again.

"Great. Remember, it's our secret. Not everyone would understand."

"Right. Our secret." I laughed to myself about her statement that not everyone would understand. I didn't know of anyone who would understand naked girls swimming and slow dancing the night away. Literally, not one person.

Chapter Twenty-six

EVEN THOUGH OUR FOOTBALL team was pretty dismal, we all tried to be supportive and attend the games regardless. Another unknown student replaced Vic Cappy as the Lancelot mascot after the stabbing incident, though obviously everyone who tried out knew who got the role. Everyone who tried out was also sworn to secrecy with the cement and missing fingers threat.

Whoever got the position next was much shorter than Vic. Because the legs on the lancer's costume dragged on the ground as he walked, they frequently tripped him, and caused him to fall face forward on to the field. The entire pep squad had to go and help Sir Lancelot to stand back up each time he fell down. It only took one game with the knight falling down eight times before that person was also relieved of duty and replaced by a taller kid. The last thing you need if your team isn't very good is your mascot face down in the dirt throughout much of the game—too hard to work up team spirit from that position.

I couldn't drive until February of my freshman year, so socializing required my parents to drive me or if I was fortunate, one of my friend's families would drive us. Getting my driver's license was the key to my freedom, so I could go anywhere, do anything, and be anyone I wanted to be, sans my parents, which sounded like absolute heaven to me. I took the test for my permit at fifteen and a half, and my dad then taught me to drive in the neighborhood and in the parking lot of Long Beach City College. I felt comfortable driving with my dad, so I figured the driving test would be similar.

The week I turned sixteen, I scheduled my driving test with an instructor at the DMV. Each driver parked their car, a tester would be assigned, get into the passenger side of your car, and then he'd have you drive around the DMV side streets to show how well you could drive and if you knew your road rules. The longer I waited, the more nervous I became. By the time I was finally assigned a tester, I was a wreck.

I drove the route as instructed, making one mistake after another while the instructor insisted on quizzing me. "How far from the corner do you begin using your signals to indicate you're going to turn? Seventy-five feet? No, a hundred feet. You must notify the DMV within seven days of selling your vehicle. Wrong, five days. When can you drive in the bike lane? When you're riding a bike!"

I just wanted the guy to shut up and let me drive. The final maneuver was to parallel park the car. After four attempts, each time with my car further from the curb, the instructor declared the test was over. He exited the car to add up my infractions and I was certain at this point, I'd failed miserably. He knocked on my window and I slowly rolled the window down to hear the bad news.

"If it was up to me, I wouldn't have passed you, but you actually passed by one point," said the instructor. "Congratulations—I guess— though I highly recommend you practice a lot more before you actually go out on the road alone. Go inside and get your photo taken and your temporary license issued." He circled my score and wrote Passed in red marker.

It all happened so fast, I thought maybe I'd heard him incorrectly. I couldn't have passed. But I did and I was ecstatic. Of course, I never mentioned to my mom that the instructor said if it had been up to him, I wouldn't have passed. I could only think of how much fun my friends and I were going to have now that I could legally drive a car.

Then my mother uttered those terrible words, "You know this means for now, no passengers in the car. No one else but Daddy and I can ride with you. You still need to practice driving a lot longer until we'll feel safe having anyone else in the car with you. You know how teenagers are. You'll be distracted and you'll kill everyone in the car. Then we'd have to get a lawyer and we'd end up losing everything we've worked so hard for."

Okay, how did we get from the excitement of me getting my driver's license to I'm going to kill multiple people, we'll have to hire a shyster lawyer, and our family will end up on the streets? Do I at least hear a, "Yeah, Susan passed her driving test?" No, we're just going to focus primarily on the dead people and large attorney fees.

"I can't believe you're telling me this now. You never said I couldn't drive my friends when I got my license. What's the point of being able to drive myself, but no one else? That's ridiculous! I passed the test and I should be able to drive. The State of California says I can drive all the people I can fit into a car legally. Why can you say I can't?" My voice was growing louder.

"You need to calm down, Susan. I didn't say you'll never be able to drive your friends; I just said until you practice more. Dad and I will decide when you're ready, not the state," replied my mom.

Why can't I live in Russia where the state decides everything? I bet Russian mothers don't argue with the state or the Kremlin about when their daughters can drive their comrades in cars. The state there says, "Yah, your daughter passed the driving test, so get outta her way, or you'll be off to vacation somewhere in Siberia." Not, "I know more than the state and she needs more practice."

Within a few weeks, my dad got my mom to relax and I could finally drive a friend in the car. Yes, that's correct. A friend. One friend. Not two or God forbid three, but one friend. I could drive one friend to the football game, or one friend to the movie and everyone else would have to get their own ride. How do you pick just one friend? It almost wasn't worth having a driver's license, in my mind.

After a few more weeks, I could finally drive three friends max. That way, according to my mom's twisted thinking, everyone was sitting by a door and could get out or crawl out the window if I crashed the car. No one would actually die in the crash, no sleazy lawyer would have to be retained, and no costly lawsuits against my family's wealth would arise. Problem solved. Even better news was my dad bought a new car, so my mom got his old one and I got the seafoam green Galaxy 500 as my very own. Yes, I had my very own wheels now.

By now, it was early spring. I was passing all of my classes with average grades except creative writing, P.E., and art, where I actually excelled and pulled in all As. Our football team came in second to last in their league and now basketball season was in full swing. Our team was apparently fairly well respected and hoops fever now infected the whole school. Lunchtime pep rallies preceded every home basketball game, which were played after school instead of Friday nights.

After seventh period, kids would hang around campus before going over to the gym to watch the game. Sometimes, if it was a game against one of our rivals, there'd be booths and activities for us prior to the game starting, and always the pep squad and cheer team leading their unenthusiastic cheers while everyone ignored them. Kids can only get just so pepped up before they start to get a little bored.

Spring also meant the end of swim team practices and meets. We'd done well this year, and I expected to be back on the team the following year. Cathy and I remained friends, though she began to get busy working out with her club team. She invited me to come to a team tryout, but volleyball season was about to begin so I declined. I did remind her I'd love to come to another swim party at her house if she gave one. She promised to invite me when she threw another.

Volleyball tryouts were the following Monday after school. Everyone had to try out, so it didn't look like the coaches only picked the same girls each year. Since I'd never played high school volleyball, I wasn't sure if I'd make the team, but I went to the girl's gym with all the other hopefuls and sat in the bleachers until my name was called.

The coach's name was Miss Vance and I thought she was not only beautiful but also funny. She would crack jokes and make everyone laugh and I was in love from the moment I saw her. This was her first coaching job and she was right out of college, meaning she wasn't more than twenty-three years old, not that much older than her players.

In groups of six, we'd take the court and play for a while as she watched us, yelling suggestions to improve our techniques. Some of the girls were terrible and a few of us were pretty good, but everyone went through the same skills tests. Passing, setting, spiking, and diving for the ball. At the end of the tryouts, Coach Vance called everyone together to explain the selection process. I was so enthralled with just looking at her, I heard very little of what was said except that the names of those chosen would be posted on the outside of the girl's gym the next morning. Nothing about the team practice before school or any girl who didn't show up for practice being kicked off the team.

Off I go Tuesday morning to check the volleyball team roster. After I bought a donut and juice and checked in with all my friends, I dropped off my rough draft in my creative writing class, and then remembered I left my new tennis shoes in the trunk of my car so went back for them. I knew I needed to hurry to the gym to see if I made the team before first period, which would start in five minutes, and the warning bell sounded as I reached the door of the girl's gym. Quickly looking down the list, I saw my name near the bottom—Susan Webb, junior varsity.

Cool, I thought, as I jogged towards first period. This was gonna be great. If you played on one of the school teams, you'd have P.E. last period so you could stay suited up and go to practice. When last period finally rolled around and I headed towards the gym, I began to run into other girls who had also made the volleyball team.

"Where were you this morning?" asked Lindy. "I expected to see you at volleyball practice."

"What volleyball practice?" I replied.

"The first team practice, you dingbat. Didn't you listen to Coach yesterday?"

"I don't know what you're talking about. What practice this morning?"

"Were you not listening at tryouts? Everyone who made the team was supposed to go to the first practice this morning before school. If you didn't show up, you're kicked off the team."

"What? I didn't hear her say that. When did she say that? Where was I?" I said, growing concerned.

"You were standing in the circle with the rest of us. Were you not listening?" Lindy asked for a second time.

"Christ, I...ah...I was daydreaming, I guess. I didn't hear any of that. What should I do?"

"You better get dressed and go talk to the coach before practice starts. Tell her you have a hearing problem or something."

I couldn't believe what Lindy was saying. I made the team, and now I'm off the team because I missed the part about practice before school, all because I was in a stupor over how hot my new coach looked. That's not easy to explain without getting into details I had no intention of sharing. Maybe hearing loss was a better angle.

Standing outside the coach's office door, I knocked softly, but she didn't look up from what she was doing. I knocked louder and cleared my throat.

"Hey, Coach, I need to talk to you."

"What do you want?" replied Miss Vance, not bothering to look up.

"I messed up. I missed practice this morning."

"Didn't notice. What's your name?" She asked me with little enthusiasm.

"Webb, Susan Webb."

"Hum. Why did you miss practice?"

"I...ah, didn't hear the part about practice before school, and getting kicked off the team if you missed it."

"So you weren't listening or you're just slow?" She asked, looking at me over her reading glasses.

"Pretty much both, Coach. Deaf and not particularly bright. Yup, that's me," I said, pointing at my head and cupping my hands behind my ears as if it was helping me hear what she was saying.

"So why should I put you back on the team if you're slow and don't hear well?"

"Maybe because I'm tall, and I block and spike well? Those skills only require height, which I have. They don't require thought or any ability to hear," I said, enjoying our banter.

"You have a valid point," she said with the slightest of a smile. "I'll see you on the court, but don't mess up again or you're off, understand?"

"I do understand, Coach, to the best of my limited ability," I said, smiling broadly. Dang she's pretty, I thought as I headed for the gym.

As summer approached, we finished the intramural volleyball league in second place. I knew I'd try out again next year, if for no other reason than it offered me the opportunity to see Coach Vance on a daily basis, which was worth all the boring time spent practicing. If I was really lucky, my junior year, not only would she be my volleyball coach, but she'd also be my P.E. teacher, so I'd get to see her twice a day.

***

Having my own car made it much more convenient to socialize on weekends. I'd pick up Vicky and Shelly and we'd go to a movie, or school functions, and other times I'd just go surfing by myself. The freedom of having my own transportation was a prayer answered; my parents had no idea where I was going or who I was going to be with.

Now that I could drive myself, there was no need to explain where I was going. My curfew was midnight, and I figured out fairly quickly into high school that if I told my mom some of the truth and a lot more that wasn't true, she felt like she knew what I was up to and with whom. I gave her lots of information about what I was supposed to do, and then did something totally different. No harm, no foul, in my mind.

Towards the end of our freshman year, Cathy Dodd threw her last all girl's pool party and invited me as she'd promised. Cathy's party crowd was always the same dozen or so of her friends. Like the last party, we all swam and played games, drank beers, got naked and danced, but this time I felt much more comfortable about the situation. I was actually starting to look forward to being with her group. I slow danced multiple times with a few girls, and I drank more beer than I should have. I drove home slowly and once home, went quietly down the pitch-black hall towards my bedroom. Then bam, I walked right into my closed bedroom door.

"God damn son of a fucking bitch," I said loudly. "Who shut the fuckin' door?" Massaging my forehead, I opened the door and turned on my bedroom light. "God, that hurt," I grumbled. Now with a splitting headache, I collapsed into bed.

The next morning, I got up and went to eat breakfast about nine. My mom came into the kitchen and just stood there. "You sounded like a drunken sailor last night, Susan, with all that cursing and shouting," she said, hands on hips accusingly.

"Why did you close my door?" I asked. "Why would I think you would close my door? I walked right into it."

"Were you drunk?" She asked in an accusatory tone.

"Drunk? Why the heck would I be drunk? You closed my bedroom door for the first time in sixteen years and you ask me if I'm drunk? Are you kidding me? Drunk?" I figured by now I'd made my point with indignation and without acknowledging that yes, I actually drank a beer at the party.

School ended and I got my first job as a junior recreations leader in a nearby city. I was so excited to be making $1.80 an hour and working six hours a day. I loved sports and kids, so it was a great summer job for me. I could go surfing before I went to work or I could go after work. I wore shorts and a red t-shirt with a badge and my new life totally jazzed me. I coached boys and girls summer leagues, played carroms, staged team water balloon fights, and did art projects. The summer went by so quickly, I felt like it had just started before it was over and we were back at school.

Chapter Twenty-seven

ELEVENTH GRADE STARTED LIKE tenth, with football team hype, pep rallies, new classes, and expanding horizons. I made the junior varsity swim team for the second time and was elated to find out that Miss Vance was indeed my regular P.E. teacher for the entire year, plus my coach for volleyball. As hard as I tried to be cool when I was around her, I continued to act goofy and I'm sure she knew I had a huge crush on her.

One time, I was walking behind her back to the equipment room with a huge mesh bag containing all the team's volleyballs. She walked through the doorway ahead of me and instead of walking through the door, I hit the doorjamb with the bag of balls and bounced backwards, ending up on the ground on my butt. I was so embarrassed I wanted to disappear. Coach just shook her head and continued walking. When I finally got the bag of balls through the locker room door, I hoped she wasn't still in the equipment room, but unfortunately, she was.

"I've never seen anyone do that before," remarked the coach.

"You haven't spent a lot of time around me. I frequently do things like that."

"What other tricks can you do?"

"I can juggle."

"There are three softballs. Show me your skills," replied the coach, pointing to the balls.

"Oh, not softballs—chainsaws." I said, now grinning.

"Be gone," she said, laughing.

"Later..." Could my life get any better? Yes, it might.

***

"Hey, Susan, guess what?" said Vicky coyly.

"You won the Publishers Clearing House Sweepstakes?" I said, acting surprised.

"You are so strange," answered Vicky. "No, I have great news. Liz is moving back to Long Beach."

"What, are you kidding me? When?"

"In two weeks, and she's enrolling at Lakewood High School."

"What happened? It's been three or four years."

"Her parents wanted to come back to be near family. I'm so excited, aren't you?"

"Yeah, really excited." What I was actually feeling was hard to describe. She was the first girl I'd ever kissed, my first love, but now my life looked much more full of possibilities than it did when we were in seventh grade. I'd met Cathy's swim team friends; I knew there were other girls who felt the same way I did. I had my own car, I surfed, and I worked my first real job. I wondered if things would be different now. I wondered if I was different now.

Many things happened over that school year. Liz did come back, but she had changed and so had I. She was now dating boys, and we never really talked about what had happened between us. She'd always wave and smile when we saw each other at school, but we never again spent any time together. Vicky told me Liz's parents had found out she liked girls and flipped out. Her parents were constantly questioning her as to whom she was with and where she was going, and she finally just gave in to acting as if she preferred boys. I understood the pressure; it was really hard to be different at our age.

I had begun to hang out with a new friend named Cindy, whom I met at the beach while surfing. She introduced me to a whole new group of her friends that attended Millikan High School, who were funny and athletic. We spent much of eleventh grade skiing and surfing on weekends and holidays. We'd ride our bikes to a neighborhood drive-in movie, sneak over a fence to turn up two or three of the speakers full blast and go back over the fence to lay on the hill in the grass and smoke weed while we watched the movie.

At one of my new friend's parties, I was showing off for some girl I found attractive and crashed someone's minibike. I thought I was being really cool by doing a wheelie, forgetting that how far back you twisted the right hand grip determined a minibike's acceleration. Meaning when I lost my balance and fell off backwards during the wheelie, my right hand was still on the accelerator and this caused the bike to jet full speed down the alley while my legs and feet dragged along the ground behind the bike.

I bounced off their neighbor's trashcans as if I was in a pinball machine until I finally crashed into a fence. By then, I had grated both of my bare feet, where they had dragged on the blacktop, to the consistency of ground beef. The girl didn't appear to be particularly impressed by either the difficulty of the bike trick or interested in nursing me back to health, because while I brushed rocks and sand out of my wounded feet, she actually left with someone else just after I hit the fence and crashed.

My friends were all howling hysterically, reenacting the event over and over throughout the evening by pretending to be driving a minibike before crashing into a wall and falling down, each time with more exaggeration, flailing arms and hilarious laughter. Unknown to me, the weed and beer masked the pain I would feel the following day.

Sunday morning, I could hardly walk, my feet were so sore. Putting on shoes was out of the question. I hoped by Monday that I could at least put on gym shoes, because we were back in volleyball season and Coach Vance would kill me if I couldn't practice. Of course, my parents wanted to know what happened to my feet, and I told them some vague story of a minibike and a wheelie. As usual, my mother went on interrogating me until I satisfied her desire to think she knew exactly what I did on weekends, before I hobbled off to my bedroom.

I was not better by Monday morning; in fact, now in addition to the ground up parts of my feet, they were very sore and my ankles very stiff. Apparently, getting dragged behind a minibike is traumatizing to feet.

Determined to get to practice that afternoon, I bandaged and wrapped gauze around my feet and painfully put them into my shoes. I limped around the halls from class to class and finally made it to P.E. There I transferred my very ground up and sore feet into my gym shoes and headed for the courts. As always, we started the session with running laps around the gym. Usually one of the faster players, it took all my energy just to jog. I played my way through the pain until the end of the practice, and finally the coach said she wanted to see me in her office after class.

"What's the problem today, Miss Webb?"

"Nothing, Coach," I said, trying not to limp as I walked.

"Something wrong with your feet?"

"No."

"You're walking weird. Take off your shoes."

I slowly untied my shoes and pulled off my socks as the Band-Aids and gauze came unsecured. I pulled the remainder of the bandages out of my socks like a magician pulls the never-ending scarfs out of his sleeve.

"What the heck? What happened to your feet?" she said, frowning, with a look of confusion.

"Remember I told you earlier that things just happen to me, or if it's gonna happen, it will be to me? Well, that's what happened."

"Okay, so *what* happened?"

"I did a wheelie on a minibike bare footed, fell off the back, scraped my feet, and crashed into a fence. That's why my feet are so sore. I knew if I missed practice you'd kick me off the team, so I decided to just try and power through the pain, as they say."

"So how's that working for you?"

"Not well at all. My feet are killing me!"

"I'm afraid to ask why you were doing a wheelie on a minibike."

"Yeah, don't ask. It just seemed like a good idea at the time."

Eleventh grade went by so fast, I was surprised when it was June and school finished for the year. I went back to my beloved recreation leader job for the summer, and I was promoted from Junior Rec Leader to Senior Rec Leader and was now making a whopping $2.40 an hour.

Chapter Twenty-eight

IN OUR SENIOR YEAR, I saw less and less of Shelly and Vicky as they moved on in their lives and I'd moved on in mine. My routine revolved around my job, skiing, swimming and volleyball practice, surfing, and my friends. The girls I hung around now liked to hike and roller skate, go to the beach, and party at anyone's house whose parents were out of town. No one was in a real relationship and we just had a blast hanging out together. I finally felt like I fit in.

Cindy had an older sister who lived in San Diego and we started going down to stay with her on the weekends. We'd sleep on her living room floor, getting up at the crack of dawn to go surfing. My brother was finishing college in Colorado, and my dad was starting to talk about retirement as soon as he got me through college. When I turned eighteen, my parents said I was on my own to make my own decisions because I was now legally—drum roll please—an adult.

Good grades had never been my priority. If I liked the classes, I did well. If I didn't, I did poorly. Overall, my grades were average—junior college, not university material—and we just happened to have one across the street from my parent's home.

I finished high school on the varsity swim team and the varsity volleyball team. I'd started playing park league volleyball at night and had been encouraged to play when I transferred to Long Beach City College. Coach Vance left my senior year to coach college volleyball in Hawaii. I was heartbroken for weeks after she announced she would be leaving, but realized I'd never see her again after I graduated, so wished her luck at her new job. We had one last exchange where she asked me to drop by her office on her last day.

Her desk had flowers, balloons, and gift boxes covering it when I knocked softly on the doorjamb.

"So you're ditching us for the big time," I said.

"Yes, definitely the big time," she replied, and smiled.

"Well, good luck. Hawaii's cool; you'll enjoy it."

"Yeah, I'm looking forward to it."

"I just wanted to tell you, Susan, that you really are a very talented athlete, and you should pursue volleyball. I think you could be very good, possibly Olympic material if you put your mind to it."

"I don't know about that. Remember, I don't hear or think too well," I said, cupping my hands again behind my ears to amplify her words and pointing at my head.

"But if you don't make the Olympic team, you can juggle chainsaws, right?"

"Yes, yes I can." I was now giggling. "And I can kinda do wheelies on a minibike."

"I'm sure you'll be just fine either way."

"Yeah, I think I'll be just fine, Coach, no matter what."

The sequel, **Find Your Heart**, begins in 1969 at junior college with Susan and her group of gay friends on the cusp of young adulthood. You'll laugh and cringe at their antics and the sometimes awkward results as the group is introduced to the gay women's bar scene, new apartments, the women's movement, and the painful struggles of their first relationships.

About Susan Stocker

Writing since I was a child growing up in Long Beach, California, I've always enjoyed making people laugh. I heard "you should be a writer" starting in grade school. Many careers later, which included graphic design, photography and social work, I have finally come full circle back to the writer phase and I love it.

I live in Claremont, California with my partner Jan, and a variety of pets on our one third acre.

We enjoy frequent international travel and are both avid photographers. We volunteer at Crossroads which is a program for woman coming out of prison. I lead a therapeutic writing group and Jan is a cooking coach.

Connect with Susan
Email susanstocker.author@gmail.com

Note to Readers:

Thank you for reading a book from Desert Palm Press. We have made every effort to edit this book. However, typos do slip in. If you find an error in the text, please email lee@desertpalmpress.com so the issue can be corrected.

We appreciate you as a reader and want to ensure you enjoy the reading process. We would like you to consider posting a review on your preferred media sites such as Amazon, Smashwords, Bella Books, Goodreads, Tumblr, Twitter, Facebook, and/or your blog or website.

For more information on upcoming releases, author interviews, contest, giveaways and more, please sign up for our newsletter and visit us as at Desert Palm Press: www.desertpalmpress.com and "Like" us on Facebook: Desert Palm Press.

Bright Blessings

www.ingramcontent.com/pod-product-compliance
Lightning Source LLC
Chambersburg PA
CBHW051123260626
47170CB00005B/1645